A Ticket to Tewkesbury

A Ticket to Tewkesbury

Neal James

PNEUMA SPRINGS PUBLISHING UK

First Published 2008
Published by Pneuma Springs Publishing

A Ticket to Tewkesbury
Copyright © 2008   Neal James
ISBN: 978-1-905809-34-9

Cover design, editing and typesetting by:
Pneuma Springs Publishing

A Subsidiary of Pneuma Springs Ltd.
7 Groveherst Road, Dartford Kent, DA1 5JD.
E: admin@pneumasprings.co.uk
W: www.pneumasprings.co.uk

A catalogue record for this book is available from the British Library.

DEDICATION

This book is dedicated to my wife Lynn, without whose patience
and support it would never have seen the light of day.

Acknowledgements

Thanks go to my daughter Lisa for her part in keeping it on track, to my son James for comic relief in times of stress, and to my future son-in-law Rob whose obsession on the subject of grammar proved invaluable.

Special thanks go to Gavin and Joyce Jones for the inspiration to begin writing, and also to Keith and Muriel Jones for unfailing appreciation and positive feedback over the past twelve months.

I am also indebted to the Storiesville on-line writers' community for their continuing support and encouragement, particularly: Max Booth III, Lori Branston, Dipankhar Dasgupta, Paul Harris, Jason Haugh, Cody Brendan Horonzy, Michelle Huff, Amie Kerlin, Jessie Masoner, David Neve, Russ Potter, Amanda Salvucci, Brandon Scott, Alexandre Sébastian, CD Walker, Nathan Weaver, Stephen West and Christian Wright.

Last but by no means least, my gratitude goes to Pneuma Springs in general and Vivian Akinpelu in particular for their guidance and advice, and for taking a chance on me.

1

*J*ulie Martin's aunt Molly was seventy-four when she died in April 1992 and it had fallen to her to take care of the old woman's affairs at the end. She'd hated doing it when her own parents passed away some years before, and the fact that Molly had been her own mother's identical twin sister didn't help matters at all. It had been like living through the whole episode once more and although her husband Doug was as supportive as he could be, he had no real idea of the emotional turmoil that she had gone through during the weeks following the funeral. As sole executor of her aunt's will it had been Julie's responsibility to ensure that all bequests and instructions were carried out, but the most difficult side to it all had been sorting through Molly's possessions. There had been all of the usual collections of memorabilia which she had accumulated, in addition to papers concerning the ownership of her house and all her savings, but the more personal items were confined to the recesses of her wardrobe, and that was where Julie found the letter.

Molly didn't have a large collection of clothing, the deprivation suffered by many British people during the war had seen to that. The culture of 'Make Do and Mend' had applied across the entire strata of society in some shape or form. Nevertheless each item was searched through before being parcelled up for a variety of charitable causes which her aunt had favoured during her lifetime. Nearing the end of her clothing 'safari', and at the conclusion of a particularly tiring day, Julie had almost missed it in her rush to get the last of the stuff away from the house. Out of the back compartment of an old handbag with a broken clasp, a letter emerged. The envelope was cream, but must have originally been white and now tarnished with age. The writing on it was in fountain pen, something quite unusual nowadays, and beautifully written in a flowing style. What made it all the more intriguing was the fact that the stamp bore the head of King George VI. Julie was no philatelist, but realised that this would make the likely date of its writing between the years 1939 and 1953. Where on earth could Molly have come across it?

She sat down on the bed and stared at the envelope in her hands. It was still sealed and bore no post mark – a fact which meant that it had therefore never arrived at its destination. There was no return address on the other side and the writing was not that of her aunt, so it must have been an item of mail which had been mislaid in the street, possibly by the person sending it, and who was on their way to the post office. That's it, they must have dropped it and Molly would have picked it up intending to post it on herself. Perhaps this intention was interrupted by some other event and she put it into her bag, intending to deal with it later. From that point in time it was probably forgotten and consigned to the back of the wardrobe along with the hand bag. Molly had been born in 1918 and Julie reasoned that she would have been at least thirty-five at the time she picked up the letter. The nagging question persisted, should she open it?

If she did, it would be abundantly clear when her aunt had come into possession of the envelope since there would have to be some date on whatever paperwork it contained, but did she have that right? On the other hand what harm could it possibly cause now, over fifty years later? What if the intended recipient were still alive? What would they say if their private mail had been read? These questions tumbled around in Julie's mind for what must have been an age, and she was only aroused from her reverie by the sound of her husband coming up the stairs, presumably in search of her. She looked at her watch and realised that she must have been musing over this piece of correspondence for almost an hour.

"There you are, thought you'd run off with the milkman!" Doug was one of those men who firmly believed that he had a sense of humour and that the rest of the world just wasn't on the right wavelength.

"You should be so lucky, have you seen the state of Stan Machin? I'd have to run backwards to even give him a chance of catching me. No,

I got distracted by this."

He took the envelope from her hand and turned it over. Even held up to the light it gave no clue as to its contents save the fact that it held a number of sheets of paper. She explained the circumstances of its discovery and was more than a little delighted when he suggested that they open it. It was, he said, highly unlikely that it held anything of great importance after forty or fifty years; anyway, he added, wasn't she just the slightest bit curious as to what was in it? Still not entirely convinced, and bearing in mind the lateness of the hour, she put it into her own pocket intending to re-examine it once they got home. Parcelling up the last of the clothing, they loaded all that could be carried into their Astra Estate ready for distribution in the morning. All of the furniture was scheduled to be collected the next day by a house clearance company for a nominal fee in readiness for putting the property up for sale at the weekend. With one last look back at a house where she had spent so many happy hours as a child, Julie bade a tearful farewell to a host of fond memories and could almost see Molly standing at the door waving her off as she had done so many times in the past. She got into the car at Doug's impatient prompting, and they drove home.

Once there, the business of preparing dinner together with unpacking the car in readiness for the next day's delivery runs overshadowed the enigma of the letter and it was once more forgotten albeit this time only very briefly. It was just as they were locking up for the night that Julie rediscovered it in her coat as she was searching for her house key. She took it back into the kitchen where Doug was finishing the washing up and placed it on the table, still unsure of the ethics of what she was about to do. Her husband turned from the sink.

"You might as well open it. After all, who's going to know if you do? There's only me, and I'm not likely to grass on you now am I?"

Needing no more prompting, and with a conscience suddenly scoured clean of all doubt, she slit the top of the envelope carefully with a knife, taking care not to damage any of the contents in the process. Doug wiped his hands and came to sit beside her at the table as the tarnished packet revealed its contents for the first time in over half a century. It smelled musty, but not unpleasant. It was the kind of smell you got from someone's front parlour which was only used on special occasions or from a chapel on Sunday school mornings.

Molly had one of those kind of rooms and they had laid her out there in time-honoured fashion as neighbours had come to pay their last respects. Two crisp pages of notepaper dropped out on to the table along with a smaller, stiffer item in the form of a railway ticket – it was one way, Grimsby to Tewkesbury.

Julie started to read the letter out loud to her husband. It was poignant in its simplicity and came from another time, now long forgotten, when everything was much simpler. It revealed the beginning of a story which had started in the midst of the worst conflict that the world had ever known, but which held out so much hope for the writer and, presumably, the receiver of its message. When she had finished and replaced the leaves of paper into the envelope, they both sat in silence for a moment almost in awe of the words of an individual almost certainly no longer alive. Those words were as fresh now as they had been when the envelope had been sealed, and Doug sat there nodding his head in silent resignation. His wife had that look on her face, which told him that she would not rest until the mystery was solved, and it would appear that there was little that he could do to stop her in the quest..

That quest would cover an almost straight line from Gloucestershire through their home in Solihull to Cleethorpes on the east coast, and Doug had his doubts as to its advisability. Despite Julie's wish to somehow 'put right' whatever wrong had been caused by her Aunt Molly's failure to post the letter, he had questioned her desire on the grounds of possibly reopening old wounds. His concern was doomed to failure as his romantic wife clearly had other ideas, and in the end he gave in.

2

'9, St Mary's Lane
Tewkesbury
Gloucestershire

1st June 1946

My Darling Maddie,

I have been able to think of nothing but you since coming back to Gloucestershire, and curse every waking moment that we are apart. Father has asked me to join him at the garage where I had started working just before war broke out, but I have not yet told either him or mother of any of my plans for the future, and he is puzzled by the hesitancy.
I fell in love with you from the moment we first met when I returned from France, and the few weeks which we spent in each other's company have convinced me that I can have no other future than with you. Please say that you will marry me and come to live here. I have taken the liberty of purchasing a rail ticket for you and it is enclosed with this letter.
Your parents were very kind to me on my visit last week, and I trust that I made a good impression. I had hoped that your father would make his decision then and there, but perhaps that was a little too much to

expect in the circumstances.

Please come to me my darling and make me the happiest man in the world.

All my undying love,

Roger.'

Roger Fretwell was eighteen when Germany invaded Poland and triggered the Second World War. He had lived a calm and stable childhood in the Gloucestershire town of Tewkesbury, and had left school at fourteen to work with his father, Graham in the family business. Graham Fretwell was a highly regarded local car mechanic and had been running a thriving business for over ten years. It had always been his intention, in the fullness of time, to hand over the reins of that business to his only son Roger, and had been at the point of doing so when fate intervened. Roger received his call-up papers at the end of 1943, served during the German attempt to break through Allied lines in the Ardennes Offensive, and was injured in the final attack on Berlin. Finding himself back in Britain towards the end of hostilities he met up with a young nurse at a rehabilitation hospital in Kent late in 1945, and instantly fell head over heels in love with her.

Madeline Colson was two years his junior and a qualified nurse at one of the hospitals reserved for the treatment of returning servicemen. At five feet seven, with auburn hair and dark brown eyes she could have charmed the birds down from the trees, and Roger's heart leapt each time his eyes fell on her. He had tried unsuccessfully on a number of occasions to put pen to paper in an attempt to reveal his feelings, but each effort had ended up as a ball of paper thrown disconsolately into the nearest waste bin. He was beginning to think that the opportunity was passing him by when fate stepped in and took a hand.

Lance Corporal Roger S. Fretwell had taken shrapnel hits when a grenade exploded to his right during a routine patrol, and although not too seriously hurt was deemed unfit to take any further part in the final onslaught on the German lines. Lying in a hospital bed in Kent, recuperating after an operation to remove the pieces of metal from his legs, he had plenty of time to contemplate his future, and Madeline had become a focus of that plan. A careless step by a fellow patient on crutches had taken the man into a collision with Roger's bed, and the impact sent a searing pain through both of his lower limbs. Madeline had been close by at the bed of another soldier and came hurrying across. Seeing Roger in obvious agony, she had administered the usual pain relief and was sitting by his side with his left hand in hers when he reopened his eyes.

The effect had been electric. They stared at each other, both transfixed for what seemed an eternity. His lips dried and his throat felt parched as he struggled for something to say. All of her professional training should have prepared her for this kind of situation, and it was well known in medical circles that recovering servicemen often formed attachments to their nurses. The spell was broken by the sudden arrival outside of a further batch of casualties from one of the Channel ports. As she pulled away, his grip on her hand tightened almost imperceptibly and she turned back to him, her face flushed with uncertainty.

"I have to go, duty calls."

"Please, say you'll come back again soon. I must speak to you, and I don't think I'll be in here for very much longer by the look of the new arrivals outside."

She smiled faintly as their fingers slowly parted, and his eyes followed her every move as she left his bedside for the doorway to the ward. Here she paused only very briefly and half turned to nod her head and then disappear. Roger Fretwell could feel the beat of his heart pounding in his ears and looked down at his shaking hands. The feelings he experienced on the front line in Belgium in 1945 were nothing in comparison to the emotions currently running through his entire being. Was this love? Was the emptiness which he now felt at her parting what his mother had told him about when she had made the knowing observation?

'You'll know our Roger. When the right girl comes along you'll know. Don't bother going looking love, fate will put you together and from then on it's all up to you. You'll only get one go at it though, so make sure that you get it right.'

Susan Fretwell had been a typical country wife and mother of the time, keeping house while her husband brought home the bacon, looking after home and children. She was a fount of wisdom in the home, and there never seemed to be a cross word between her and Graham in all the years that Roger knew them. It had given him a loving and stable background, and now this nurse, this perfectly formed being who had invaded his consciousness had apparently arrived to fulfil the prophesy. He must not let her slip through his fingers, this could be his only chance at happiness and he would have to strike while the iron was hot.

He didn't see Madeline again that day, and lay awake for most of the night worrying in case that had been his only chance. When word arrived the next morning that she had been called away home unexpectedly on family business, he was almost in despair. The next few days were the worst he could ever remember in his life, and the medical staff were becoming quite worried that his current condition was somehow linked to the injuries which he had sustained. He had suffered a relapse, of that there was no doubt, and for a number of days was in a feverish state until an infection in one of his legs succumbed to treatment. It was on the Friday evening that his condition stabilised sufficiently for him to regain consciousness. The first thing he saw when his eyes opened was Madeline.

It was at that point that he got to know her name, and a relationship started to grow and blossom within the confines and strict rules of the hospital. She took him out into the grounds in a wheelchair when the weather was fine, but it was always in the company of other patients, and his only consolation was that she made sure that he was the last one to be returned to the ward. On one of these 'private' moments he seized the opportunity to tell her how he felt. It was now or never, and with his legs now getting strong enough for him to walk unaided, an imminent departure for home was on the cards.

"Stop the chair please."

"Why, is there something wrong?"

"Yes nurse, there is. I can't go on like this. It's tearing me apart having you around and not telling you how I feel."

"Oh dear, I think I know what you are going to say."

"I am in love with you Madeline. Oh, may I call you Madeline? Please don't think badly of me, I know this isn't supposed to happen but I can't help how I feel. I've been mad about you since the first day I saw you. Do you, could you, love me?"

She flushed and sat down on a nearby bench where she parked the chair. She clasped her hands on her lap and stared out into the distance. Pulling her cape around her shoulders for warmth as the temperature seemed to have dropped suddenly, she looked into his eyes and smiled a smile which he hoped he would remember until his dying day.

"I thought you would never ask, and when I had to go home suddenly I was worried that the moment might have passed, and that you may even be gone when I returned."

"Does this mean that we're engaged to be married? I mean, will you be my wife?"

"I'll have to speak to my mother and father before I can give you an answer, and then you'll probably have to formally ask daddy yourself. Write your address down for me before you leave and I'll get in touch."

By the end of the following week he was back in Tewkesbury and discussing his stay in Kent with his father and mother. They were understandably delighted that he had found someone and were looking forward to meeting Madeline.

3

Madeline Colson's upbringing had been in one of the more prosperous suburbs of Britain's major fishing port – Grimsby. Her father and grandfather had owned and run the largest fishing fleet on the East Coast, and her life had been one of genteel comfort amongst the upper classes of the town. They lived in an imposing detached house on Queen's Parade in Cleethorpes away from the hustle and bustle of the docks with all their smells of fish. She had attended the local girls' grammar school and had progressed to the Royal College of Nursing on the back of some excellent results in her end of school examinations. To say that the family were proud of her achievements would have been stating the obvious, and Madeline's father Thomas Colson entertained high hopes for his daughter's future.

Madeline's mother, Dorothy Nelson, was the daughter of a Derbyshire colliery owner who had made his money during the inter war years as industry re-equipped itself for domestic production once more. They had met during a summer holiday which she had spent at a nearby resort, and with the agreement of both sets of parents had married that autumn. Thomas Colson was undeniably the head of the household, and whilst not an overbearing or unreasonable man, he ran the family as he ran his firm and expected that life would continue its course along the path clearly laid down.

When Madeline was first summoned home it was to the bedside of her maternal grandmother who had contracted a severe chill whilst out with friends. She had taken the opportunity to let it be known that she had caught the eye of a young soldier who had returned home from the front, and that a romantic attachment was forming between them. Like most fathers, Thomas Colson was initially happy that his daughter had taken the first steps on the way to 'settling down'. Whilst not overly disapproving of the female sex going out to work, he was nevertheless a firm believer in how he saw the structure of the typical family, clearly regarding Madeline's excursion into the world of nursing as a useful component of her future as a wife and mother.

It was after tea on the Saturday afternoon of her next visit that a more detailed discussion arose around the subject of her fledgling attachment to Roger Fretwell. Once the army uniform had been stripped away, what sketchy details that were known of his background came to the fore, and the more Madeline talked the fewer were the facts that she realised she knew about her new found love. That he was the only son of a Gloucestershire couple she was well aware, as was the fact that his chosen career would be that of a mechanic. It was at this point that Thomas Colson began to become a little uneasy at the direction in which his daughter was moving, and he attempted to point out to her, very gently, that the step which she was proposing was a big one. That she knew very little about her young admirer was very clear, and to his mind a romantic attachment of some permanence was an inadvisable step at this time.

His concern took a more serious turn when it emerged that Roger Fretwell's only ambition lay in taking over what was, it had to be said, a small family business within a rural and somewhat unsophisticated setting. He pointed out to his daughter, amid her increasingly emotional state, that the expense which he and Dorothy had laid out on her education should not be wasted in some West Country backwater. Whilst not standing in the way of Madeline's happiness he nevertheless regretted that his daughter had even considered a union to a family so clearly beneath her in social standing. Mindful of the likely actions which young people are apt to take when their preferred choice is denied them, Thomas Colson stepped back from specifically forbidding a relationship with the young soldier. He did, however extract from her an undertaking to seriously consider the likely outcome of his marriage proposal before taking any further steps in that direction.

That this was not the unanimous verdict of the Colson household was made evident to Madeline some while later on the same day, when a conversation instigated by her mother caught the nurse completely by surprise. Thomas Colson was, she stated, a snob. A very nice natured snob it had to be said, but a snob at heart. He valued his social standing within the local community as an employer and was, as a number of local charitable organisations would testify, an altruistic individual prepared to contribute some small part of his personal wealth to those less fortunate. Unhappily this did not seem to include his own family. Dorothy told her daughter that her own father had held much the same opinion of 'that smelly fisherman' when they were 'walking out', as it was called in those days. Thomas Colson had been 'a bit rough around the edges' for her parents in the beginning, but as time passed they saw in him what she had seen, and came to appreciate his good points whilst tolerating those of a more rustic character.

It was important, she said, that Madeline be sure in her own mind of the course which she intended her life to take, and that if it involved Roger Fretwell, so be it. She would never be turned away by her family, and her father would simply come to terms with something which he had no chance of preventing. He was a man of much bluster but no malice, and treated in the correct manner, could be manipulated into the appropriate way of thinking in the end. Madeline smiled amidst her tears. Dorothy Colson had such a simple and straightforward outlook on life, and could always be relied upon to come up with some solution to the knottiest of problems. She had not given her blessing to Roger Fretwell, and would withhold such an action until a time when she had met him face to face, but for her daughter the day seemed suddenly much brighter and she was now impatient for her return to Kent and the man who had stolen her heart.

Although she had prepared herself for the fact that the young soldier may not be still at the hospital when she came back from Lincolnshire, Madeline was nevertheless disappointed to find his bed empty upon her return. Enquiries with other staff revealed that she had missed him by only one day, and that he had left a note for her in the matron's office. Unfortunately for the young nurse it was to be the following day before the head of the nursing staff returned, and she was horrified to discover that, although the note had indeed been handed to the matron, it seemed to have been lost. Despite a concerted search of the office, nothing resembling it was forthcoming. Without the message Madeline would have no idea of Roger's address and since all details of returning servicemen were held by the appropriate regiments, she had no means of contacting him unless he made the first move.

To say that she was distraught would be to oversimplify an emotional situation. Madeline retired to her room at the end of the day and cried herself to sleep. There would be nothing for her to do but wait, and in waiting lay the dilemma. Would her silence be misinterpreted by him as a cooling in her feelings? Would he think that she had been toying with him all along? What would her parents think of the situation after all that she had told them about him? What on earth was she going to do?

In the event, matters were somewhat taken out of her hands by a larger than anticipated arrival of battle weary and injured troops from the continent. With fighting intensifying as Germany's resistance crumbled towards its eventual capitulation, there would be little time for her to ponder her personal situation, and the weeks following on from Roger's departure were extremely busy ones for all of the staff at the hospital. She had made efforts to discover his address, but with the Ministry of War and the regimental authorities concentrating on matters of far greater significance, her requests went unheeded. By the time that the conflict was over and her duties in Kent had eased, six months had passed since the day of her return from her home in Lincolnshire and Roger's return to Gloucestershire. In all of that time there had been no word from him and consequently no means of obtaining any idea of his whereabouts.

Once back in Cleethorpes and working at a local medical establishment, her father's advice had been that of the intensely practical man that he was. She should get on with her life and whatever career she saw fit to pursue until marriage came along, and forget all about the young soldier. Fate had decreed, he said, that their romance was destined not to flourish and that she ought to be grateful that it had not progressed any further. Dorothy was more sympathetic, being a romantic at heart, and secretly worried for her daughter's happiness – Madeline had seemed so certain that this man was the one for her, and even as a child she had never been one given to making leaps of blind faith.

4

*A*unt Molly had always wanted her final resting place to be back in the town where she had been born and had grown up. She had left Tewkesbury in 1938 at the age of twenty when she married Leonard Smith, and went to live with him and his family in Solihull where they spent a very happy and contented life until his death in 1990. She had grown to love the area and had made many friends during their marriage, her only regret being their lack of any children. She had come to regard this as a stroke of fate and typical of the age, had taken a philosophical stance of 'Que Sera' – it was just not meant to be. His parting at the age of sixty-nine had left her with a wealth of memories, and her remaining years were spent amongst a host of well-meaning friends and neighbours. Julie had not realised just what this had meant until the day of the funeral when the church was packed to the rafters.

The journey down to the West Country was largely uneventful, and with their two children left in the more than willing hands of Doug's parents they had taken the opportunity to spend a rare day out together. Once out of the immediate area of Solihull, the Hearse speeded up and made good time, arriving in the Gloucestershire town within an hour and a half. Calling first at the vicarage of St Michaels they were greeted by the Reverend David Tomkins, who accompanied them to the nearby church where a private service and interment had been planned. Word had obviously got around of Molly's return and Julie was pleasantly surprised to see a dozen or more elderly residents awaiting their arrival. They had all been school friends of her aunt and had come to pay their last respects and share a few memories of her for the last time.

In the clear blue sky of an early summer afternoon, with the breeze gently swaying the treetops as if in some final farewell wave, Aunt Molly was laid to rest in a corner of the churchyard where she had tended the graves of her parents in years past. Fresh tears were unashamedly wiped away from ageing eyes as the small party made their way out of the church grounds and back to their separate homes. Doug and Julie politely declined several offers of refreshment, wishing to get back home before evening and, shaking the hand of the vicar once more, returned to their car. Once inside the vehicle, Julie pulled from her bag the letter which she had found in Molly's wardrobe.

"You didn't."

"I did, and it would be a shame not to try to find the place as we're so close."

"What if there's no-one there who knows him? What if the place no longer exists?"

"We'll never know if we don't take a look, now will we?"

It was pointless to even attempt to reason with her when she had the bit between her teeth and with a resigned shrug of the shoulders Doug put the car into gear and they moved off to find someone who could direct them to the address at the top of the first page. They didn't have to go far before Julie spotted the post office.

"Stop here Doug, they'll know in there."

The postmaster was relatively new to the area, but pointed them in the direction of the River Avon and a row of cottages on St Mary's lane, a distance of around half a mile. Julie smiled her thanks to the man and was back in the car before Doug had time to think. They pulled up in a gravelled area set aside for the residents of the riverside properties and Julie was taken aback by the sheer beauty of the spot. Small wonder it was that Molly had wished to return to the place, it was all peace and tranquillity.

The cottages stood a little way back from the bank of the river, each with its own fairly small but neatly tended front garden, and a ginger cat was sunning itself on the broad window sill of one of the properties. An old man was busy pottering around the flower beds which surrounded an immaculate lawn, and he paused in his labours, curious to see two visitors in a place where strangers were something of a rarity. Leaning on his hoe, he removed a handkerchief from his pocket, tipped back his cap and dabbed away the perspiration from his brow as they approached. Julie had never been the shy type so she went forward and introduced herself and Doug as relatives of Molly Brown; the man's faced brightened in recognition of the name.

"You'd best come inside for a spot of tea then. Ma will have the kettle on."

They followed him inside the cottage and sat down in the back parlour out of the glare of the sunshine. It was a room straight out of the 1950s with all of the chintzy paraphernalia typical of the time. In addition to the stout oak table and regulation four chairs, the furniture was supplemented by a large Welsh Dresser against the outside wall, a small decorative table which held a Dansette radio still in full working order and a large ornate sideboard from which the lady of the house was now removing a set of what looked like her best china. The floor was one of stone flags covered by a central carpet of Oriental design, and the centrepiece was a large coal fireplace and range where, the man said, they still did all of their cooking. As if in confirmation of that fact, a brilliantly shiny kettle was now singing away to itself on one of the hobs turned inwards to the fire. The old man took it off and poured the boiling water into a large brown teapot.

"So, you're relatives of Molly are you? Seems like just yesterday that she got wed and moved up to the Midlands. We didn't go to the church; you don't want too many gawping when putting somebody in the ground, do you?"

He introduced himself as Sam, nothing else just Sam. His wife was 'Ma' and they had been married for over forty years. They had lived in the cottage all of that time, and he had been at school with Molly since 'infants'. Over the course of the next hour or so, and against all their initial intentions of getting back home, Julie and Doug enjoyed the open hospitality of Sam and his wife and relaxed in the easy and comfortable atmosphere of their cottage, which had seemingly become trapped in a kind of time warp. Julie had become caught up in the euphoria of the place and completely lost track of the time. Doug being Doug had simply sat back and listened to the couple's life story as it unfolded before him. He had heard it all before of course from his own father, and was not surprised to find similarities between the tales he was now being told.

Seeing the afternoon rapidly turning to dusk, Julie was suddenly on her feet and apologising for taking up so much of the couple's time. They had, she said, to get back home to rescue her husband's poor long-suffering parents from the ravages of their two children. Thanking Sam and his wife for their hospitality, they made their way back to the car and after a prolonged spell of waving, were on their way back to the M5 and the fairly short trip home. As Doug had expected, his wife was soon asleep as was her manner on such journeys and with the radio for company he put his foot down, eased off the entry slip road, joined the motorway and headed north.

Right on the button, Julie was awake as soon as they pulled on to his parents' drive and into the house to find out what havoc their two children had wreaked during the day. It had been nothing like that of course and never was, but the standing joke had to be played out like some old gramophone record. They sat down for the penultimate cup of the day and Julie draped her coat over the back of one of the chairs in the lounge. Out of the right hand pocket fell a small cream coloured envelope, and she stood there staring at it in dismay. Doug of course thought it extremely funny.

"I don't believe it! All that time and I completely forgot to ask him about Roger Fretwell. Do you think we should..........."

"No, I don't. If you think I'm driving all that way again, you're madder than I ever believed." Doug was smiling, but she was in no doubt that her one opportunity had now gone – he was home, and firmly intended to remain there.

Never one to give up without a fight however, Julie was not finished with the matter and even now was planning the next stage in her campaign to get to the bottom of the message which her aunt had been hiding for the last forty years. The east coast was, she had heard, a very pleasant place to be in summer.

5

Sam and Ma waved the young couple off and stood at the end of the front yard watching as the Astra disappeared from sight at the end of the lane which led to the row of cottages. It had been a very pleasant end to the day and he had been ready for a sit down following his ritual afternoon in the garden. In truth there was very little that needed to be done on a regular basis, but he had always believed in keeping active and was convinced that this policy was the main reason for the apparent health and heartiness of both he and his wife. At seventy-three and seventy-one respectively their appearance belied the age which they had both attained, and the only regular disruption to the idyllic life which they led was the periodic invasion of grandchildren who added colour to their already active existence. Sam scratched his head as he and his wife turned to go indoors.

"Bit of a rum do that, weren't it? I wonder what brought them all the way down here."

"Just passing by I suppose." Ma replied "Probably spotted the river and came down for a look. Nice couple though."

"Nah." Sam shook his head. "Wonder if they were looking at George's old place up at the end. Too far to come just on the off chance. Bet the agent sent them down here. I didn't see which way they came from until she walked up to the gate."

"You could be right. Place like this would be just right for children. Wonder how old theirs are. Come on, let's get inside and have a bit of supper, it's dropping a bit chilly now, and you're no spring chicken you know."

Sam laughed and gave her a gentle shove as he fastened the gate. Inside the cottage the kettle was once more whistling away at the only tune it knew, and Ma was putting out the crockery for a cold supper of ham and pork pie. Tommy, their ginger cat, was prowling around her feet in anticipation of any morsels which 'accidentally' fell on to the floor prior to taking up his usual position in front of the fire for the rest of the evening. Conversation over supper continued on the subject Julie and Doug, and it was Ma who kept it going when Sam appeared to be prepared to let the subject die.

"You ever get one of those feelings when something unexpected happens and there doesn't seem to be any reason for it?"

"You've been reading too many books, missus. What are you on about?"

"Her, the young woman. You said she came up to you."

"I did."

"Well it must have been for a reason, and she never made any mention of George's place that I heard. I'm sure that there was something that she wanted to know, but she never seemed to get round to it. Must have been all your nattering that put her off."

"Cheeky beggar, pass the teapot. It couldn't have been so important if she never got around to mentioning it, but now you say that there was something odd about them. I mean coming down here to bury a relative's one thing, but stopping off at the home of complete strangers like us is something else. You don't just go for a stroll after a funeral and turn up on somebody's doorstep like that for no reason at all."

This conversation played itself back and forth during the rest of the evening, as would any new subject in the lives of a rural couple with limited exposure to the greater world outside their own existence. The personalities of Julie and Doug Martin were dissected and examined in minute detail both as strangers and, in Ma's opinion, potential neighbours until the two pensioners were satisfied that no further information could be gleaned from the short visit that afternoon. Convinced at this point that the couple were merely possible purchasers of the house at the end of the row which had formerly been occupied by the now deceased George Murfin, Sam and Ma gave the matter no more thought that evening and retired to bed.

It wasn't until a few days later whilst out shopping for their weekly necessities that they had occasion to call in at the post office. As with many small settlements there are a number of establishments which form the backbone of the local community and typically these would include, to varying degrees of personal importance, the church, the local pub and the corner shop. Having no corner shop as such, the post office served a dual function for those in the neighbourhood, and in addition to being the conduit for exchange of gossip, it also boasted a small area containing a few tables where afternoon teas were served. In this way it acted as a magnet for those veterans of the locality whose families had grown up and left the area. Today was no exception and the usual gathering was present discussing such weighty matters as the price of potatoes, the vicar and the young couple who appeared out of nowhere to bring dear Molly Brown home (God rest her soul).

Sam had not been listening particularly closely to this morsel of tittle tattle, but Ma's ears were more finely tuned than those of her husband, and her internal radar system was now focussed on the voice of Mrs Hancock and the news which she was imparting to the assembled guests.

"Yes, they just turned up, bold as brass and asked my Eric where St Mary's Lane was. Bit of a cheek if you ask me. Never bought a single thing whilst they were in here they didn't. I says to him, Eric I says, there's a price for information and it don't come cheap. You should have sold them something while they were in here. How else are we going to pay our bills?"

"So who were they?" This from a stout little woman with a Pekinese contentedly lapping tea from a saucer on the table top.

"Blowed if I know, and Eric never thought to ask. I mean, what are men for if they can't be relied on for information? They just upped and left in their car towards the river."

"What did they want then, does your Eric know that?" Interest from a feather hat fresh from the greeting card stand pushed the conversation in another direction.

"Well, and this is the interesting bit, seems they were looking for someone living in one of those cottages down there. Sam, that's one in you row isn't it?"

Sam never got the chance to answer, not that he would have got involved anyway, and Ma stepped into the spotlight much to Mrs Hancock's annoyance. They were, she said, a very nice young couple from Birmingham way. They had young children that they'd left with grandparents for the day whilst they came down here to bury dear Molly Brown (God rest her soul). It was Ma's considered opinion that they were looking to buy old George Murfin's house and move down here with their lovely family.

Eric appeared at this point and, like a fish out of water in the midst of this meeting of the local gossip society, opened his mouth before putting his brain into gear and ended up wishing that he hadn't bothered.

"That can't be right. The address on the envelope she had wasn't his at all, and she pointed at it when she asked me for directions."

"So whose was it then?" The lady of the house - now indignant that her thunder had been stolen not only by one of her regulars, but had also been neatly packaged up and despatched by her own husband.

"Didn't rightly see." Eric was now sidling carefully towards the door to their private quarters, hoping to extricate himself from the hole into which he had dug himself.

The fact that he escaped further interrogation was due only to his wife's being interrupted by the Pekinese knocking the saucer from the table, and the sudden crash of breaking pottery concealed his disappearance. The short journey back home was one of some reflection for Sam and Ma as they mulled over the information which had been divulged by Eric the postmaster. If they were wrong about George's house, what had been the reason for the young couple's visit? The woman, Julie, had some sort of letter but was it to be delivered, or had it been found and if so, by whom? There were four other cottages in the row, but it would be bad manners in the extreme to go knocking on doors prying into the private lives of others. Eric hadn't seen the address clearly enough for a house number to be apparent, but the fact that Julie had approached their house puzzled them. Could the letter have anything to do with him or Ma?

6

*I*f Doug had thought that the matter of the letter had been quietly forgotten he really should have known better, and the issue was duly resurrected during the summer when they arrived at their holiday destination during the six week school break. The first hint that he ought to have been aware of, and which should have set some alarms bells ringing, was that at no time had there been any discussion of a likely venue for the two week stay. Accommodation was never the issue, as they had purchased some years before a four berth caravan, so booking anything in advance had not been necessary as they had been regulars at a number of sites along the east coast. One telephone call during the week prior to departure had been sufficient to guarantee their reservation.

Their children, Elizabeth and James, had always enjoyed the caravan holidays and the freedom it gave them from dawn until dusk each day without having to stick to fixed routines of mealtimes. This year Julie had, for reasons kept very quietly to herself, chosen Cleethorpes as their preferred destination. It had not dawned upon Doug until they began their unpacking that there may have been an altogether different reason from normal for the selection of that particular place. Julie had been hoping to keep quiet about her ulterior motives until a little later in the two week stay, but in lifting one of the suitcases on to the top of a wardrobe Doug inadvertently knocked her handbag off the bed. The entire contents went cascading across the floor and he cursed himself for his clumsiness. Julie took great pride in the order in which she kept things in her bag, and he would have to try and re-sort the contents now.

He never ceased to be amazed at exactly how much his wife could cram into the Tardis of her bag, and recalled an instance at the Imperial War Museum in London when a fresh faced young policeman asked to inspect its contents as a security measure. To Julie's eternal embarrassment, and amongst all the usual paraphernalia, out came a pink cotton shortie nightie which she had hurriedly stashed inside it once their suitcases had been consigned to the boot of their car. A cream coloured item on the floor suddenly caught his eye, and putting the rest of the rescued contents on to the bed, he picked it up. He had to smile, it was the letter sent by the young soldier to the nurse fifty years ago, and now he understood why they were in Cleethorpes. At that precise moment his wife entered the room.

"What's all the noise Doug? Ah, so you found it. I was going to mention it later today, love."

Doug smiled. It was impossible to be angry with Julie no matter what she did, and he resigned himself to a day in the company of his very own Sherlock Holmes as she followed the trail of the elusive young couple to the home of Madeline's father just off the sea front drive. For the moment however, that could wait as the children were impatient to get to the beach and the sea which they both swore that they had never seen before in their lives. Packing up buckets and spades together with all the other absolute necessities, they headed off for the south end of the promenade which also boasted a fair ground and swimming pool along with the ubiquitous crazy golf course.

Julie, of course, would take all of this with a pinch of salt, select a deck chair and go and sit right out of the way with the daily paper. Such was life.

Although keen to resume the quest for the destination of the letter which had now been in her possession for the better part of three months, it was not until the Thursday following their arrival on the east coast that Julie had ventured to suggest to the rest of the family that they go in search of the Colson property on Queens Drive. Doug had remained philosophical about his wife's campaign and the children had become caught up in the excitement of what they saw as a piece of detective work, so it was little wonder that they found themselves parked up on the Central Promenade near the pier just after lunch that day. Bribery in the form of a game of crazy golf on the course just off the Sea Road one way system had taken care of Elizabeth and James' needs for the moment, and the stroll towards the Bawtry Road was over in around half an hour.

After a pleasant lunch at the Lifeboat pub on the corner of Queens Parade and Kingsway, the family made their way along the former to its junction with Oxford Street where a large corner plot contained the imposing dwelling place of the family of Madeline Colson. It was a large double fronted Edwardian villa sitting in the back right hand corner with elegantly structured gardens to the left and front. The driveway was partially concealed by a mature shrubbery which ensured a level of privacy for the dwelling. Ensuring that she had, in fact, got the correct address Julie led her family up the gravelled drive to a large porch and rang the bell, half expecting a liveried servant to answer the summons, and was pleasantly surprised when an immaculately dressed woman in her mid forties opened the door.

"I'm so sorry to bother you, but we are trying to trace a family whom we believe lived here at one time before the war. My name is Julie Martin; this is my husband Doug and our children Elizabeth and James. We're here on holiday until Saturday week and I wondered if you had any information as to their whereabouts."

"That would have been the Colsons. Would you like to come inside, I've just made tea and we could sit in the conservatory and talk. I'm Miranda Farnley."

Julie had not expected to find any immediate reference to Madeline's parents at such an early point, and accepted the offer without hesitation. Access to the conservatory at the left hand side of the house was down the wide and elegant hallway which served the entire property from front to rear. It was cool in the heat of the early afternoon, and the shaded conservatory was furnished with cane chairs and a variety of tropical plants. Over tea and a selection of cream cakes, Miranda introduced her husband Gregory who had just returned from a round of golf at his club.

"The Colsons were a wealthy and much respected family around here, but when the regulations governing fishing fleet sizes and catch quotas came in, the trade declined considerably and they were forced into selling off the majority of the trawlers towards the end of the 1980s. The company itself no longer exists following the death of the last surviving son in 1984, and this house is the last evidence of their presence around here."

"I suppose it's a sadly familiar story around the whole country." Julie sighed and would have made excuses to leave had Miranda not taken the conversation in an unexpected direction.

"Pardon my asking, but what is your interest in the family?"

Julie looked at Doug for inspiration but having anticipated the glance; he was taking an inordinate interest in the views across the garden and silently ignored her pleas for help. She turned back to Miranda and opened her handbag.

"I found a letter amongst the possessions of my late aunt, and the trail led us from Solihull to Tewkesbury, and then on to here. I suppose I'm being nosey but I don't understand what connection there may have been to the writer and recipient. My dear husband thinks I'm mad, but the whole thing has stirred my curiosity."

"May I take a look?"

"Of course, it's only a photocopy and it isn't ours, but we've read it several times. I don't suppose it will cause any harm now."

Miranda read Roger Fretwell's romantic plea to his Madeline and passed it on to her husband. Was that a tear Julie notice in the corner of her eye as she turned away? They sat in silence as Gregory smiled his way through the pages, folding them carefully and returning them to the envelope. Julie was certain that her hostess was on the point of saying something and held her breath in anticipation. It was not to be however, and after a few more exchanged pleasantries they made their way back to the front door and said their farewells. With mounting disappointment Julie accompanied her family back along Queen's Drive and on to a promised visit to the amusement arcades beyond the pier, when a call from behind them halted their progress.

"Mrs Martin………….." Miranda came hurrying along the street.

"Julie, please."

"Julie. Gregory and I feel that there are things that you need to know about that letter. There is more to this matter than a mere romance, and we would like to talk to you both again tomorrow if it's convenient."

Doug and the children had returned down the street to the two women by this time, and arrangements were made to meet again the following day back at the former Colson residence. Miranda's parting comment took them all completely by surprise, and Julie in particular was stunned by the revelation.

"Miranda Farnley is my married name, but I'm the granddaughter of Thomas Colson and the house was left to me in his will. The letter that you showed to us was destined for his daughter Madeline. She is my aunt and when my mother died some years ago she was my last surviving relative assuming, that is, that she is still alive."

As they made their way back to the sea front, Julie couldn't help wondering about Miranda's revelation of her connection to Madeline. If those tears were not real it would make the woman one hell of a good actress.

7

With the children now happily involved in a game of indoor ten pin bowling at one of the myriad of amusement arcades along the northern end of the promenade, Julie and Doug bought refreshments and sat at the side of the lanes. From a simple case of tracing the family of some unknown nurse at the end of the Second World War, the matter had now deepened into something akin to a minor mystery, and the question to be answered was one of whether or not they felt the inclination to become involved any further. Doug had tried to distance himself from the latest of his wife's 'treasure hunts' but was beginning to feel strangely intrigued by the nature of their latest discovery – Miranda Farnley. Whether she actually spoke for her husband when revealing a little of the family history to Julie remained to be seen, and they could hardly have been so rude as to decline out of hand the polite offer of a further discussion of the matter – after all it was they who had turned up on the Farnley's doorstep without so much as an introduction.

Julie had been unusually quiet about the conversation with Miranda, and Doug had learned long ago to leave her alone with her thoughts at such times. Collecting Elizabeth and James at the end of their game, the family moved on further up the promenade to the large indoor Market in search of some holiday 'bargains' which they knew could be obtained from closer to home at reduced prices, but which kept their children entertained after a fair amount of walking. Several hot dogs and an ice cream later, they were on their way back to the car when Julie spoke up.

"We know very little about this family Doug, and it might be a good idea to get some background on them before we meet up again."

"Ok, so what do you have in mind?"

"Let's find out where the library is. They're bound to have some local history information, and I'm sure it won't take long."

With the bribe of a fish and chip meal, the children were more than happy to go along with Julie's suggestion of an hour at the library. Both were avid readers and the prospect of a fresh set of books to browse through revived their flagging interests. The building, situated at the corner of Albert Road and Alexandra Road was a single story open plan structure offering a cool reservoir from the midday heat, and the two children disappeared into its shady depths immediately leaving Julie and Doug to make their enquiries at the desk. The librarian was a very helpful woman in her mid fifties who pointed them in the direction of a well-stocked local history section and a set of tables and chairs for study. It didn't take Julie very long to find just what she needed – a soft back A4 booklet produced by the local historical society containing biographies of all the major local dignitaries and personalities. With Doug happily occupying himself in the science fiction section, she sat down to read.

The Colsons had indeed been well-known and respected amongst the community, and had risen to prominence as a result of Thomas Colson's skill as an entrepreneur in the fishing industry. He had married Dorothy Nelson, the daughter of a Derbyshire Colliery owner, in 1918 and they had three children, Susan, Roland and Madeline. Roland died in 1984 as a single man, but Susan married Stephen Wilkinson a local builder in 1946. Madeline Colson, the final child, was the subject of the letter in Julie's possession, and although Miranda had said that this woman was her sole surviving blood relative, there was no mention of her amongst the names of the Wilkinson family. Julie read and re-read the section of the booklet a number of times and, finally giving in, asking the librarian for any further information on the subject. The woman frowned and shook her head, but suddenly brightened as a well-dressed man came through the front door of the building.

"Why don't you ask Tom Skerritt" she said, pointing in the man's direction, "He's the one who researched and wrote the booklet. If anyone knows, he will."

Julie approached a tall, silver haired gentleman in his seventies as he hung up his coat just inside the library door. He smiled as any author would upon meeting a reader of their work, and accompanied her back to the table where her 'research' lay spread out. She introduced herself, and having explained the reason for her search, Julie went on to relate the circumstances of the letter which had been the trigger for her investigation, and Tom nodded his head in silent agreement.

"Once you've got the bug for digging around it never really leaves you. What was it that you needed to know? I assume it has something to do with one of our esteemed local families."

"Yes, the Colsons. Your text seems to cover the entire family history since the late nineteenth century, but I came across someone claiming to be a granddaughter today and yet she doesn't appear in any of your writings."

"A granddaughter?" He frowned, "I'm afraid that's not possible because the family line died out with Roland in 1984. Susan was the only one of the three children to marry but she certainly had no offspring. You must be mistaken."

"She said her name was Miranda" Julie continued, "And she's actually living at the old family house on Queen's Drive with her husband Gregory. She also claimed to be the niece of Madeline Colson, the woman I am trying to trace."

To Tom Skerritt, this was one more of life's mysteries, and his hobby as local historian had certainly provided him with his fair share of those. Nevertheless, his research had always been meticulous and he had acquired a reputation for leaving no stone unturned in his 'excavations' into local notables. To find this stranger so adamant in her findings might have severely irritated a younger man, but something about Julie told him that there was more to this than a mere error of judgement.

"Would you mind terribly if I took a look at the letter? I'm sure that you really believe what you've been told, and I'm more than a little curious as to the reason why someone might try to mislead you."

Doug had returned from his safari amongst the nether regions of deep space and time machines, and Julie introduced him to Tom. She pulled the letter from her bag, and handed it over. Tom Skerritt took more than a few moments studying the outside cover of the envelope and taking the pages out, laid it carefully down on the table.

"That's certainly the address of the Colson family home, and the stamp's authentic for the date at the top of the letter. Did the woman you spoke to ask you for this?"

Julie was sensing that Tom Skerritt had more about him than a person of historical leanings, and told him that Miranda had read the contents several times before handing it back to her.

"There's no address at the top and it's a photocopy. Is there a reason for that?"

"Just a fancy I had I'm afraid. We tried to find the location some months ago, but there was no time for more than a cursory visit. I just felt that it wouldn't be right to show the original to a complete a stranger. You never know who you're talking to do you?"

Tom Skerritt's face had changed significantly from that of the pleasant gentleman who had strolled into the library not thirty minutes earlier. He now wore the furrowed brow and serious expression of a senior policeman on one of the popular T.V. crime dramas. He stroked his chin several times as he leaned back in the chair. Doug had taken a seat opposite and was now hanging on every word of the conversation. It seemed for just a brief moment that time itself had stood still – Julie always did say that he read too many Asimov books.

"Have you arranged to meet this woman again by any chance?"

"Well she did invite us back to the house tomorrow, and we sort of agreed to go. Is there a problem with that?"

"Only if she knows where to find you. I would advise against returning there until I've had the chance to do some digging around. There are a few people I need to talk to. Don't tell me where you are staying, but come back here the day after tomorrow at three, and we'll talk again. Until then I'd advice staying away from Queen's drive if you can manage it."

With that he stood up, shook them both by the hand and left the building. Rounding up two protesting children, Julie and Doug headed back to their car and drove the three miles to the camp site where they had parked the caravan. That evening, with Elizabeth and James tucked up in bed, they talked about Tom Skerritt for the first time since the afternoon.

"What do you make of him then?" Doug was now quite interested for the first time in a matter which had initially bored him to tears.

"The whole thing sounds a bit odd if you ask me. Why pretend to be a Colson if you're not? What could she possibly hope to gain from a love letter fifty years old? It was such a blatant lie, but we wouldn't even have found out if we hadn't run into Tom Skerritt, and I'm not sure what to make of him."

"Well there's nothing to be gained until we see him again, and he didn't try to get any more information from us did he? I mean he even said he didn't want to know where we were staying. Let's sleep on it; we'll take the kids to Mablethorpe tomorrow."

8

*T*om Skerritt hadn't always been a jolly old man, and despite his outward appearance of being every child's favourite uncle, beneath the surface of his genial countenance there lurked a cold, calculating nature. He had seen and done the kinds of things that are best kept away from members of the general public, and whilst loyalty to his country was unswerving he would not hesitate to take the most radical action should circumstances demand it. Such a set of circumstances had now presented themselves to him, and he had a clear course of action to follow. Picking up his telephone, he dialled a number which does not appear in any official listings. He spoke only one word.

"Fostropp"

"You found them?" The voice was that of a person of similar age to himself

"Maybe. I'll know more tomorrow."

"Are they aware of you?"

"No, our librarian friend pointed a young woman in my direction. It was pure chance."

"What have you got?"

"A copy of a letter written in 1946. It's addressed to the Colson house and the young woman and her family have already been there."

"Do they know what's involved?"

"No, and Miranda has arranged to see her again tomorrow, but I told them not to go back until I have spoken to them again. It's under control."

"This family, where are they from?"

"The Birmingham area I believe, and before you ask they have already tried unsuccessfully to locate the people we're looking for."

"Good. That means that there'll be no repercussions at that end. We don't want them going missing again now that we seem to be so close. Don't make any moves in that direction until I give the go ahead."

"Alright. I'll be in touch again in a few days when I know more about what's happening at Queen's Drive."

Replacing the receiver, he filled his pipe with Erinmore, struck a match and sat down with a single malt to consider his plans for the following day. Removing a hard backed book from a safe in the wall of his study, Skerritt wrote down the details of the events of the afternoon, together with a transcript of the telephone conversation. Reading through what he had committed to paper, he nodded and replaced the document into its hiding place, securing the door afterwards. He had hoped that after so much time the case would have been quietly consigned to the archives. It had seemed so very important at the time, and he was a much younger man then. All of this cloak and dagger stuff was not the kind of thing which he thought he would still be getting involved in during his retirement.

Skerritt needed to gain the Martins' total confidence and convince them that his was the only way to proceed with the discovery which Julie had made. The fact that Miranda Farnley had got to them first did not appear to have caused much of a problem at the moment, but any further communication between her and Julie could compromise his task in finding the author of the letter. He could not allow the Farnleys that advantage, and the failure of a mission which was now forty-five years old simply did not bear thinking about. He had enough information at his disposal to discredit Miranda and her husband, and although the majority of it was true there was always the chance that any lies may be exposed at some point further down the line. That in itself would not be too critical the closer he got to his target, but a false move now would certainly ruin everything.

The trick would be in knowing how much to tell to Julie and her husband without scaring them away before he had the original letter in his possession. His concentration was broken by a knocking at the front door, and he was surprised to see the librarian standing inside the porch. She had come directly to him the moment the library had closed, and handed over two cards bearing names and addresses.

"Temporary membership cards, Tom. They've taken books out for the children and I asked them to fill them in. I thought you might be interested in their whereabouts and I got them to put down both their local and home addresses."

Tom smiled and thanked her. Maisie could always be relied upon and her anticipation of his needs was, at times, simply uncanny. He showed her to the door having copied the details into a notepad, and returned to his study to clear away the material which he had be reading at his desk. In one single moment, he had been placed in a position where he would be able track down the Martins when they returned home. All that he now needed to do was to convince them of the danger of any further communication with the couple at Queen's Drive, and if years of service to his country could not provide him with that ability, then he may just as well hang up his spurs.

He needed to get his hands on the original copy of the letter, and certain that Julie would not be stupid enough to carry it around with her all the time, the skills of a fellow expert would be required to obtain it for him. Picking up the telephone once more he dialled a local number and a young woman answered at the other end.

"Hello June didn't expect you to be there, is your dad in?"

"Uncle Tommy, how nice to hear from you. I was just on my way home, but hold on I'll get him for you."

"Tom?" The voice of a man of slightly younger age than Skerritt came booming down the line.

"Yes. Look where are you off to Bert? I need to see you urgently and it's not something I'd like to discuss on the phone."

"Ok, get down to the Lynton on Taylor's Avenue in about half an hour, and I'll meet you there. Back in business are we?"

"Possibly, depends on what we find. I'll see you there."

Bertram Peterson had served in the same army regiment as Skerritt and they had been through a number of post war campaigns together. A bond of absolute trust had built up between the two men and they had served the needs of their country on several occasions in the intervening period. He was sitting nursing a pint when Skerritt walked in, and emptied the glass in readiness for a refill.

"Ok, what's the big secret Tom?"

"I need something lifted from a caravan just outside of town, and the details are on this piece of paper." He slid a note across the table and Peterson picked it up.

"That all, a letter? By the way you were talking I thought it was something far more serious. What is it, naughty husband?"

"No, there's much more to it than that kind of thing. We've been looking for the man who wrote it for quite some time, and without the address there's no chance of finding him."

"What about the occupier of the van?"

"I can keep them busy for as long as it takes, and I'm going to arrange to meet them tomorrow. All I need to do is set the time to suit you, but it's vital that no-one knows you've been in there. The plot number's on the bottom of the note, so you won't need the car registration number"

"How long have we known each other?" Peterson snorted "Nothing will be out of place by the time I've finished, but I'll need a couple of hours, and I'm not going in there in daylight."

"Alright, I think I can manage to keep them away. Shall we say around ten o'clock? I'll take them out for something to eat. The woman's got a nose for a mystery, and I can spin this one out to keep her interested until you've done. Make sure to call me on the mobile when you leave and I'll wind the evening up. It'll take them around half an hour to get back and you'll be long gone by then."

As they made their separate ways homewards, Skerritt knew that if the document were in the van Peterson would find it, and there would not be so much as a speck of dust out of place to betray his presence. All he had to do now was to make up a credible story for Julie to swallow, and prevent her from contacting the Farnleys again.

9

Miranda Farnley had waited patiently all day for Julie to contact her, and with no means of locating the Martin family, she had little option but to leave the woman's obvious curiosity to get the better of her. It was now early evening and the likelihood of any communication was evaporating rapidly as the evening shades brought an end to an otherwise pleasant day. Gregory had been his usual impatient and annoying self, and was absolutely no use at all in situations like this. They had both almost given up all hope of tracking down Madeline Colson when the Martins arrived out of the blue, and Greg had immediately gone off on one of his periods of frenetic activity.

"Ring Control right away, and tell them that we have something on the case!"

It had taken her a full hour to calm him down and make him realise that this may be just one more wild goose chase. Gregory had been the cause of too many of those in the past, and Control had warned him on a number of occasions about the effect that was likely to have upon his position in the organisation.

"No, we wait. The last thing we need is to scare her away if she has the information we need." She told him, and he went off to sulk in the conservatory.

Roger Fretwell and Madeline Colson had disappeared off the radar not long after the end of the Second World War, and the address he had left as his place of domicile just didn't exist. All that was known was that he was, at that time, located somewhere in the South West of England and may even be living under an assumed name. With Roland Colson dying in 1984 the final family contact had been lost, but even before that he had proven incommunicative about his sister's whereabouts. There had been some falling out years before and it had resulted in him and Madeline parting on less than convivial terms. If they were still alive they would by now be in their seventies, so relieving them of the information which they held should not be too much of a problem.

If that information were to get into the 'wrong' hands the consequences for the Farnleys and everyone like them would be very serious. There had to be some way of finding the Martins, Cleethorpes wasn't exactly London. She had to think. What would she do if she was doubtful of a story spun out to her by a stranger? Check it out – but where? What place, freely available, would hold the kind of information she would need to either verify or discount a set of facts? Of course, the local library. Historical societies are famous for littering libraries with booklets about local characters and their activities, and Miranda just happened to have a contact who spent the better part of each of her days reading through the piles of magazines which were strewn about the place. Anyone out of the ordinary turning up there would automatically attract her attention. She picked up the phone.

"Dilys? It's Miranda dear, family alright? Yes I suppose it could be better, how is John's lumbago? Oh dear, that's a shame. Look love I just wondered, have you noticed any strangers at the library in the last day or two? You have? Oh excellent! I'll be round in a while and we'll have a nice cup of tea while you tell me all about it."

Dilys Conrad was one of those people you would call a busybody. She had the habit of involving herself in the affairs of others when that sort of close attention was not really welcome. An inveterate gossip monger, she also tended to embellish what she had heard in order to enhance its interest when she passed it on, and this had occasionally brought her to grief with the more forthright of her circle of friends. Miranda was well aware of the woman's shortcomings, and took care in not allowing anything of importance to reach her ears wherever possible. As a result, the flow of information was virtually all one way and today's tit-bit would provide the woman with very little room to add her own slant on the matter.

Sitting in the lounge of the Conrad's first floor flat overlooking the mouth of the River Humber, the two women exchanged the customary small talk, and Miranda had to sit through the problems surrounding John Conrad's long term back problem, their daughter's unhappy marriage and the financial difficulties which both matters were causing the family. Consequently it was over an hour before the conversation could be steered into the direction which was the sole reason for her flying visit. Dilys' eyes were as sharp as needles and she missed absolutely nothing when she was about town. Julie and her family had triggered her attention purely and simply because they were strangers. The Birmingham accent had acted like a magnet to her ears, and the contents of the magazine which she had been reading suddenly vanished to the back of her mind as she homed in on the conversation about Queen's Drive between Julie and the librarian.

Once Dilys was into her stride there was no stopping or short cutting her, and Miranda had to bide her time until something of importance popped out of the monologue. That 'something' appeared in the form of Tom Skerritt, who was well-known in the area for his work in the field of local history. What made him all the more interesting was the fact that both Miranda and her husband were aware of his background within the armed forces in his younger days, and also of his retirement occupation of 'listener' for a number of departments within the security services. The start of a conversation between him and the Martins on the subject of the Colsons had been picked up by Dilys, but was incomplete due to their removal to the rear of the room.

This in itself did not unduly bother Miranda, although Dilys was irritated at her inability to complete the story and the need to embellish it with some fiction of her own. Skerritt would know that there was no family link between the Farnleys and the Colsons and would probably have made Julie aware of that fact, thus explaining her failure to return to the house as promised. Now caught out in a lie, Miranda would have no access to the Martins for retrieving the letter and an address for Madeline. With no means of discovering where the family lived, the only option left to her and Gregory would be to actually follow them home when they left the area. Fortunately Julie had mentioned the name of the camp site when they met, and with most holiday accommodation setting a ten o'clock deadline for vacating they could arrange to be in their car waiting for the family to make a move.

Exactly what Miranda intended to do once they all arrived back in the West Midlands she was not yet sure, but there was certainly no point in just sitting around in Lincolnshire sucking her thumb. Once in the Birmingham area she would at least have something concrete to report to Control, and it would then be up to them to make a decision regarding any further action. Skerritt was a name which had cropped up in a number of their files in the past, and whilst no attempt had yet been made by those in authority to restrict or terminate his activities, there would come a time when his actions became more of a liability than a source of information. The issue surrounding Madeline and Roger Fretwell may be just enough to tip that balance, and it would be Gregory's turn to do the dirty work this time.

Sensing Dilys at the end of her speech, or at least on the point of gathering her breath for another onslaught, Miranda seized the chance to disengage herself from the woman.

"Goodness me, look at the time! Greg will be wondering where I've got to, must dash Dilys dear. Look, keep in touch and if you hear any more over the next week or so please give me call. It's so nice to sit and have a chat about things."

All this was said 'on the hoof' as Miranda gathered up her belongings and hurried to the door, closely followed by her informant friend who was still pouring forth a stream of inconsequential miscellany.

"Well, 'bye then and thanks for the tea". Closing the door and making her way down the steps, Miranda heaved a sigh of relief as she stepped out on to Kingsway and returned to her car on Haigh Street.

10

*T*om Skerritt had to decide how much to reveal to Julie and her husband in order to retain their interest, whilst still keeping the actual facts of Roger and Madeline's disappearance under sufficient wraps to ensure that the documents in their possession remained confidential. There was no doubt in his mind that he had enough information at his disposal to spin out a tale plausible enough to hold the attention of an audience, and he was a story teller of sufficient skill to guarantee that he could delay the Martins' return to the caravan long enough to enable Bert to accomplish the task set for him. After an hour or two spent looking through the case notes which he had kept on the matter, he made a call to the mobile number which Julie had given him.

"Mrs Martin? Hello, it's Tom Skerritt from the library the other day. Oh good, I'm glad you remembered. I wondered if it would be convenient to see you and your husband this evening for a discussion about the Colsons. Well I thought dinner would be appropriate, my treat of course and bring those lovely children of yours along too. Well there's a nice pub/restaurant on Taylor's Avenue; it's called The Lynton, and the menu is quite extensive. Right I'll see you all there at around eight-thirty then? Cheerio."

Having finalised the meeting, all that now remained was to acquaint Bert Peterson with the arrangements in order that he could carry out his part of the evening's business. Another call, and quite a different conversation.

"Ok Bert, I've set them up for a meal with me at The Lynton at around eight-thirty tonight. I can string it out for a couple of hours and if you're in there when we arrive, there should be plenty of time to get to the campsite and carry out the search by the time we're done. Ring me when you're about to leave the caravan and I'll make some story up about the phone call."

Petersen had become accustomed to Tom Skerritt's 'little jobs' over the years and had always managed to remain undetected in his forays into the personal lives of those into whom he had been sent to enquire. Consequently, using a number of different guises he had been able to gain entry into a wide variety of properties, obtain whatever it was that Skerritt had needed, and remove himself unseen and without leaving any trace that he had been there. Tonight, with the summer season in full flow, no-one would notice one more holiday maker in suitable attire for the season walking through a campsite late in the evening. He would have to change clothes after leaving The Lynton of course, he was well known there, and seated in a corner wearing shorts, sandals and a peaked cap would cause quite a stir amongst the regulars.

Now that arrangements had been made for the evening, Tom Skerritt filled the intervening time by taking a look at any comings and goings at the former residence of the Colsons on Queen's Drive. Having seen Miranda leave in some haste in mid afternoon, he followed her to the home of Dilys Conrad and sat on one of the promenade benches with his newspaper whilst she was inside. Dilys' reputation as a bit of a 'hawk-eye' preceded her wherever she went, and Tom had been aware of her ability for spotting and recording the unusual for many years. Undoubtedly she would have noted his conversation with Julie Martin at the library, where she seemed to spend most of her time avoiding the presence of that layabout husband of hers. That Miranda Farnley had paid what was an unscheduled visit was curious, since it was common knowledge that she couldn't stand the woman.

There was no other way in or out of the flats, and Tom resigned himself to a lengthy wait for Miranda's reappearance. He took out his pipe, filled it with Erinmore and folded the newspaper at the crossword page. With two targets for his attention now, Miranda and the daily cryptic, he failed to notice the blue Mondeo as it pulled up along the promenade in one of the parking bays. The man inside made no attempt to get out but merely sat there, watching.

Gregory Farnley played a poor second fiddle to his wife's activities within the organisation, and over the years had been given little opportunity to display his loyalty and abilities to fellow members. Miranda had kept him on a very short leash, well aware of his impetuousness and unpredictability whilst being grateful for the financial clout which his family name provided for her to realise the ambitions which she harboured. He had seen and recognised Tom Skerritt outside their home and was concerned when the man turned his car around and followed Miranda on her journey. Acting quickly he pulled the Mondeo out into traffic and made after Skerritt as he disappeared at the end of Queen's Drive. Miranda had given no clue as to the purpose of her journey and she did this with irritating regularity. This could be his chance to show how useful he was, since she clearly had no idea that she was being followed.

Sitting in the car now, and watching as the watcher watched, he briefly considered the impact of eliminating Skerritt once and for all from their activities. A simple hit and run would take care of the old man, and the road was not exactly the busiest in town. Still, it would be just his luck to be seen and identified, and police involvement would infuriate Miranda. No, that was something which he could never countenance – his wife's temper was not something which he willingly encountered. A tapping on the car window jerked him out of his thoughts, and a glance to the left revealed the presence of one of the town's army of traffic wardens.

"Double yellow mate, you can't stop here. You'll have to move along or I'll be issuing a ticket if you're still here when I come back in a few minutes."

Gregory scowled. Tin pot official, nothing better to do with his time than wind up the innocent motorist. Starting the car and cursing his luck, he glanced over his shoulder for any oncoming traffic and was pulling out whilst turning back to face the front when Tom Skerritt stepped out into the road in front of him. He was not travelling fast, but had covered the thirty or forty feet without realising how far he had gone. The warden had seen the accident coming and banged his fist on the car bonnet as it passed him. By the time Gregory saw Skerritt he was only a few feet away and the emergency stop brought them to within inches of each other. The old man stepped out of the path of the now stationery vehicle and calmly came around to the driver's side.

"You want to be more careful with your driving, sonny. One day you might not be so lucky – wouldn't want somebody like me on your conscience would you?"

He took a long, hard look at Farnley. Until now he had had only the vaguest idea of what the man looked like, all of his attention having previously been focussed upon the brains of the outfit, Miranda. Smiling in a sinisterly polite manner, he completed his crossing of the road and, catching sight of his quarry turning the corner, hurried along after her. The warden, having now caught up with the car, gave Gregory his own advice on accident prevention and shook his head in resignation as the Mondeo pulled away with a screech of tyres. Once around the block he picked up his wife's trail as she headed back home, but with his curiosity now stirred he was determined to find out what Skerritt was up to.

He followed the man home at a respectable distance and waited out of sight to see what his next move would be. By the time of Skerritt's scheduled appointment with the Martins, Gregory had almost given up hope but when he saw the family pull into the car park of The Lynton his attention brightened. It positively sparkled when, a few moments later, he observed the figure of Bert Peterson leave the place in something of a hurry. That Peterson and Skerritt were what Miranda would call 'associates' had been known to them both for a while, and the man's obvious haste to be somewhere else persuaded Gregory that time could be well spent in finding out just what he was up to.

Arriving back home later that night, Gregory was faced with his wife's anger at not finding him at home when she returned that afternoon, and it took him quite a while to calm her down before he was able to tell her what he had discovered. It had been so easy to intercept Peterson as he emerged from the caravan site and returned to his car in the poorly lit street where he had left it. A sharp blow to the side of the head had rendered the man unconscious, and the removal of all his possessions made the whole thing look like a straightforward mugging. The items obtained included the digital camera which had been used to photograph the letter that Peterson had discovered, and which now revealed, Gregory hoped, the location of Roger Fretwell and Madeline Colson. Miranda smiled sweetly at her husband and patted him gently on the cheek.

"Good boy" she said "You're learning at last!"

11

*T*om Skerritt had glanced at his watch several times since ten-thirty and was becoming a little concerned at the deafening silence from Bert Peterson. It was now getting on for ten to eleven and the Martin children, as all youngsters do when they are tired, were becoming increasingly restless and clearly needed to be making their way home. Having already delayed the family's departure on one occasion, he could not risk upsetting their good nature by suggesting another drink. Reluctantly, and with a sense of misgiving, he bade his farewell and watched as they left The Lynton. Once they were clear of the premises, he pulled out his mobile phone and pressed Peterson's speed dial key. For what seemed an age, the number rang and he was on the point of cancelling the call when an unfamiliar voice answered at the other end.

"Hello, who's calling?"

"I'm trying to contact Bert Peterson. Who is that please?"

"Detective Sergeant Lawson. Who are you?"

The conversation carried on for a while as both parties established who they were and how the phone had come into the possession of the local police. Skerritt was told that Bert had been taken to the hospital on Scartho Road after being found unconscious near the Haven holiday camp site; it appeared that he had been mugged. Bert's family were at the hospital when Tom arrived and although Peterson was in no immediate danger, they were clearly upset at what had happened and no-one seemed to know why he would be in that particular area of town at that hour. Feigning ignorance, Skerritt decided that until he had the chance to talk to his friend alone and in private, there would be no point in exposing himself to any questioning by either the police or the Peterson family. He remained silent.

The attending doctor told them all that Bert would be kept in for twenty-four hours under observation. Apart from a minor cut resulting from the blow he had sustained to his head, there did not appear to be any serious injury which was causing them concern. Assuming that the police would be wanting to speak to his friend as soon as he regained consciousness, Skerritt said goodbye to the Peterson family and asked that they get Bert to ring him when he returned home. For the moment, whatever had been removed from the caravan was in the hands of other parties, and a nagging feeling at the back of his mind was telling Tom that Miranda Farnley may have something to do with it.

For Julie and Doug Martin the evening had been a mixture of the pleasantries of a meal coupled with an intriguing story going back five decades. Tom Skerritt, the local historian, was a puzzle. Julie had a feeling since their first meeting that the man knew more than he was letting on, and his carefully crafted story concerning the circumstances of Madeline Colson's disappearance didn't really satisfy her curiosity. When pressed for detail he was evasive in a very jovial way, choosing to take the narrative down his own particular chosen path. He was specific, however, in his warning on the subject of Miranda and Gregory Farnley.

Whilst no specific charges could be laid at their door it was, he said, very strange that they should choose to tell such an obvious lie about their background and its connection to the Colson family. His own interest was, of course, merely that of an amateur local historian interested only in maintaining the integrity of archive material concerning local people and places. Madeline had left the Lincolnshire area following the end of the war, and it was rumoured locally that she had travelled to be with and marry a serviceman whom she had met in the Home Counties. There had been some family falling out over the matter and despite the efforts of her father, Thomas Colson, to prevent the union the strong-minded young woman had left the family home for that of her lover.

Back at the caravan, and with the children now fast asleep, Doug and

Julie found themselves oddly deflated by what appeared to be a story with loose ends which had little meaning for them. They had only Skerritt's word for it that the Farnleys were people to be avoided and Julie in particular had felt uneasy at missing their promised return visit to Queen's Drive. She picked up the cream envelope from the mantelpiece; perhaps she had missed something in the letter, some clue as to Roger Fretwell's real intentions.

"Doug, have you read this letter since yesterday?" Julie held up the envelope as her husband came out of the kitchen area.

"No why, something wrong?"

"Just check around the van for anything missing or out of place. I think we've had a visitor."

"What on earth do you mean? It getting late you know, you sure you're OK?"

"I'm not joking Doug. I put this letter back in the envelope with the leaves' edges downwards. They were face up when I picked it up just now."

Doug knew when his wife wasn't joking, and now was one of those instances. Over the next hour they turned the caravan upside down and inside out, but everything was where it should be and there was nothing missing as far as either of them could ascertain. The door had not been forced and the lock showed no sign of being tampered with. All of the windows were secured, just as they left them every time they went out. If someone had broken in they had taken great care to try to conceal their activities. All except for the letter that is, and yet it was still there in its proper place, but upside down.

Julie's thoughts returned to Tom Skerritt's warning about Miranda and Gregory, but her visit to the site manager's office revealed nothing apart from the fact that he had been in all evening and had seen no-one enter or leave apart from holiday makers. She was just leaving when he called her back. There was, he said, one chap who looked a little out of place, but it had slipped his mind. Coming back from the site shop at around ten thirty he passed a man going in the opposite direction and walking with his head down beneath a peaked cap. The evening was turning chilly, and the fact that he was wearing open toed sandals and shorts did not seem sensible. He was no youngster either, which made the whole thing slightly ridiculous, and the Martins' caravan lay in the direction from which he had been walking.

Julie returned to the van and relayed the conversation to her husband. Doug was all for calling in the local police, but she shook her head and told him that it would be a pointless exercise.

"What would we tell them? 'We believe someone broke into our caravan whilst we were out and didn't take anything'? No, I can't imagine them being too impressed with that, Doug. Someone's been after that letter though, I'm sure of it."

"Well if it was an opportunist break-in, whoever did it was certainly taking a risk. What about this bloke that the site manager saw?"

"He couldn't describe him beyond what clothing he had on, but it's funny that he was leaving just before we got back."

"Alright, let's assume that it wasn't just someone who just happened along at the right time. Who else knew that we were going to be away from the van tonight?"

They came to the same conclusion almost immediately, Tom Skerritt. It was he who called them, he who set up the evening meeting, and he who delayed them by organising an evening meal followed by drinks. They even allowed themselves to be persuaded into one final round before leaving The Lynton, and left to their own devices would have been back home at least an hour earlier than they were; anyone still in the van at the time would have got the shock of their lives. This now left them with the problem of not knowing who to trust, and Doug was all for packing up the van and going home. Julie however, pragmatic as ever, refused to let the events spoil the holiday for the children.

"We'll tell the site manager what we think has happened, and let him make the decision about the police. In any case that letter isn't leaving our sight from now on. Somebody obviously thinks it important enough to risk their being caught."

In the event, the manager was less than enthusiastic about involving the constabulary. It was more than his job was worth for the site to gain a less than secure reputation at the height of the holiday season, and the last thing he needed was some investigator from head office snooping around. He had one or two things of his own on the go which he would rather didn't come to the attention of his bosses. He offered the Martins a refund on their second week in exchange for silence.

12

One week later, and with the issue of the attack on Bert Peterson now largely a matter of an unsolved street robbery, Tom Skerritt considered it safe to pay the man a visit and assess what had come out of the trip to the Martins' caravan. He was alone in the house, his daughter having returned home after one of her daily visits to ensure that he was alright, and the two friends moved out into the back garden where they could talk in relative privacy.

"So what happened last week then?" Skerritt came straight to the point.

"Not sure. I was in and out of the caravan in about an hour and a half. Didn't leave a stick out of place, and I found the letter you were on about behind the clock on the mantelpiece."

"Great, where is it?"

"I'm not daft enough to bring it with me; that would have let them know someone had been in whilst they were out, and how would that have made you look? You were the one who persuaded them to leave the place for the evening. No, I took the digital camera along and got half a dozen images."

"Alright, so where's the camera? Oh God, don't tell me it got nicked when the mugger hit you."

"I'm afraid it did, but whoever took it got just that. There was no memory card inside it. That little baby was safely tucked inside one of my socks so the photos I took are safe and sound."

"I should have known better. What have you done with the card?"

"Safely downloaded on to my laptop, and the images are as clear as a bell. I took close-ups as well, so that you would get a good reproduction of the address. It's all here, look I'll boot it up and you can see for yourself."

True to his word, Bert had five or six beautifully clear shots of the envelope and its contents, and now that Skerritt knew Fretwell's home to be in Tewkesbury he would be off there at the earliest opportunity. If the attack on Bert had really been a simple case of a mugging there was nothing for Tom to worry about but if, as he suspected, the Farnleys had something to do with it, time would not be on his side. They would make another attempt to retrieve the letter once they had found the camera to be empty.

Miranda Farnley had been furious when she discovered Peterson's camera contained no memory card, and cursed Gregory for his carelessness in not checking the thing before leaving the scene. They had both returned to the edge of the camp site during the early part of the week to assess the possibility of gaining entry to the van for themselves, but Julie had been too clever for that. Unwilling to leave it unguarded any longer, she had persuaded the site manager to allow Doug to move it directly opposite his office. This, she had said, would be part of the price of his carelessness in not making the area secure. Miranda's only hope of now finding the letter lay in following the family back home at the end of the week and organising a raid on the house at the earliest opportunity, and for that she would need some of the experts which control had at its disposal. She decided to tell them nothing of the current fiasco.

The Martins had kept well clear of Cleethorpes since the evening of their meeting with Skerritt, getting up early each morning and taking the car to a variety of other locations within the immediate area. It was clear to Julie that there was a considerable amount of subterfuge between Tom Skerritt and the Farnleys, and that it had something to do with the letter written to Madeline Colson by Roger Fretwell. Unless there was some coded message lying within the text, it appeared to be nothing more than a simple love letter between two sweethearts separated at the end of the war. By the time Friday evening came along, all the bags were packed and loaded into the car ready for a very early start the following day, and with the site manager now relieved to see them go they pulled off at five o'clock that morning. When the Farnleys arrived at the site some three hours later they were well on their way back to Birmingham.

Back at Queen's Drive following the abortive trip to the caravan, Gregory made himself scarce and retreated to the tranquillity of his golf club where he spent the rest of the day. Miranda fumed her way around the house, cursing in the emptiness and damning her husband for his crass stupidity. She would now have to reveal the whole story to control and let them come up with a solution to the situation. It was a telephone call which she was not looking forward to, after building up a network of contacts and listening posts over the past ten years. All that could be lost if those at the top decided to replace the unit with fresh faces. The voice at the other end was its usual soulless tone, devoid of any emotion and the background echo sent a chill down her spine.

"So what you are telling me is that your source as now vanished, you have now idea where they are except for the fact that they are living somewhere in the vicinity of the second largest city in the UK, and that the information which we require is not in your possession. Is that correct or am I missing something?"

"No, that's about it. To be fair to Greg, he had no way of knowing that the camera was empty at the time he took it, and the fact that he acted on initiative to rescue a situation which was being taken out of our control by Skerritt must weigh in his favour."

"We are not talking 'fair' Miranda, the matter is one of the utmost importance to our organisation. If the information which Fretwell holds becomes public we are all finished. You do understand that do you not?"

"I do, and we intended to follow the Martins when they left the camp site, but by the time we arrived they had already gone. The site manager proved less than informative although I'm sure he would have some record of their home address."

The man at the other end sighed impatiently. Miranda was a good agent, of that there was no doubt, and she had served the cause very well for a number of years. It had to be said however, that of late Gregory had become something of a liability and all her efforts to keep him under control had come to nothing. It was never easy when a contact had to be terminated, but with so many young and enthusiastic recruits coming through the system it was increasingly difficult to justify the retaining of an inefficient unit. He made a note to instruct the 'clean up' squad; the Farnleys would be going on an extended vacation very soon.

"Alright. We will have to organise a visit to the Peterson home. I trust you have the address?"

"Yes, I'll e-mail it to you right away."

"Good. You and Gregory stay out of the picture for now. I will contact you again once there is more positive news on the subject."

Killing the call to his mobile, he immediately dialled another number and ordered in a 'Retrieval Squad' to obtain the information from Peterson's camera immediately. One further call to the 'Travel Agency' and arrangements were made for the Farnleys to take an 'all expenses paid' holiday to some far away place on the following morning. The house would be cleared of all that could link it to the organisation and a sale arranged with a local estate agent. The removal of an established unit always left a bad taste in the mouth and had never been his favourite task, but in a job like his it was very much a case of dog eat dog, and given that choice he really had no option. Making a note in the daily log, he closed down his laptop and put it back into the carrying case, picked up his coat and left the office.

It was seven o'clock – much later than he had planned and in all likelihood dinner would be spoiled once more, much to the annoyance of his long-suffering wife. Stepping outside the Metropolitan Police HQ at New Scotland Yard and into the evening sunshine, he took a deep breath and headed for the tube station at St James' Park for the short journey home.

13

With no-one but himself to bother about, Tom Skerritt's time was very much his own and a brief call to his neighbour to ask that an eye be kept on the house for a few days ensured that nothing would go amiss whilst he was away. Martha, the aforementioned friend, missed very little that happened in the locality and was utterly reliable in all matters of nosey neigbourliness. He packed a few essential items into a small overnight bag and set off for the other side of the country the day after his meeting with Bert Peterson. The man had wanted to come along, but Tom managed to talk him out of it on the basis of his continued recuperation. The fewer people knew about the circumstances surrounding the letter the easier it would be for Skerritt to put the matter to bed once and for all. It had been seven-thirty when he left Cleethorpes faced with a two hundred mile trip, and turning on to Tewkebury's market place four hours later he looked around for a likely source of information.

Stepping into the same post office which the Martins had used months before, he was greeted by Eric Hancock the postmaster. Showing him the address which he had on the copy of the letter supplied by Bert Peterson, Tom was curious at the man's puzzled expression as he glanced at the details. He looked Skerritt up and down with a frown upon his face and handed the paper back to him.

"What d'you want that address for?" He asked, still smarting from his wife's continual reminders of his earlier incompetence.

"I have some friends in the area, and that's where they live. I'm a stranger here, and it would take me ages to find it on my own."

"Can't you ring them?"

"No telephone I'm afraid, they're odd like that. Prefer to live life the simple way and sometimes I can't blame them."

"Well it's just…………." He never finished. Out of the back room, like a galleon in full sail, his wife steered her way imperiously between the counter and the newspaper stand.

"Eric! What did we say about information? Has a price, it does we said, didn't we? Shouldn't be given away free should it? Time's money and free information don't earn us anything." She stood arms akimbo like some Sumo wrestler waiting for the first move.

"I'll take a newspaper please, I didn't get chance to pick one up before leaving home." Skerritt smiled at the postmaster's obvious discomfort "And you better let me have a tin of Erinmore Ready Rubbed as well. I seem to have run out."

Now placated, Mrs Hancock retreated to their private quarters once more, leaving the connecting door wide open just in case her husband gave away any more morsels of 'chargeable' gossip to passing visitors.

"Come outside and I'll show you the way. Let me know when you're going back home and I'll parcel her up for you to take with you." He jabbed a thumb over his shoulder at the location of his ensnarement.

"Thanks, but I think I'll pass on your kind offer. I tried marriage once and it gave me the most awful indigestion."

The postmaster directed Skerritt out of the town centre and along the road travelled by the Martins down to the river. He waved in resignation at another failed attempt to free himself from the clutches of his dear wife. Head down and shoulders hunched, he returned to the shop and another joyful day in the company of the local busybodies who were gathering for their lunchtime feast on the current subjects of the local gossip. He would refrain from divulging the subject of the visitor's enquiry to assembled crowd; there were some things you just didn't want to get involved in and another humiliating session at the hands of his wife was more than he would be able to bear.

Tom Skerrit pulled up in the same car parking area which Julie had used earlier in the year, and marvelled at the beauty of the scenery in this little backwater of the small town. Unlike before however, there was no-one about in any of the gardens and with no identifying numbers on any of the front doors, he would just have to take pot luck and pick the first one in the row. Opening the white planked gate, he strolled up the garden path to be greeted by a large ginger tom which had been sunning itself on the wide sill of the left hand window. The door was slightly open, presumably for the cat's convenience, and knocking on the door frame he heard the slow, measured approach of old feet encased in carpet slippers as they 'swooshed' their way across a stone flagged floor. The white haired man in his seventies shaded his eyes against the bright sunlight and struggled to identify the shadowy form of the stranger before him. His countenance changed significantly when the familiar soft voice addressed him.

"Roger, my dear man, how have you been all of these years? When was it that we last met, forty-six I believe?"

Skerritt had an eye for detail and a good memory for faces. No amount of denial from the man before him would persuade him that he was anyone other than Lance Corporal Roger Samuel Fretwell, late of Her Majesty's armed forces and holder of the Military Cross for bravery in the face of the enemy during the Ardennes Offensive in Belgium.

"So, what do you want Skerritt? Is this you just passing through and thought you'd look up an old friend?"

"If only it were as simple as that Roger. No, it's taken quite a while to track you down, and if it hadn't been for a chance meeting with a young couple who were down here at the start of the summer, we wouldn't be having this conversation now. It's the package I've come for."

Roger Fretwell waved Skerritt inside and they sat down in the same front room which had served them during the afternoon chat with the Martins. There was much to catch up on since the signing of the German surrender in 1945, and although not an afternoon of soldierly recollections the two men had many things in common. They both had been involved in the final push towards Berlin and had run across each other in the aftermath of the collapse following Hitler's suicide in the bunker. That was when Fretwell had stumbled across a German wearing the uniform of the Führer's senior staff. The man was thick set, of medium height and had brown straight hair combed backwards from his brow. When challenged, he dropped the briefcases which he had been carrying and disappeared amongst the rubble of the capital. Roger never saw him again, but picking up the cases he was startled to see, embossed upon the leather of the front flap of one of them, the initials 'M.B.' In the years following the collapse and rebuilding of the German state, there had been many alleged sightings of Hitler's private secretary but Martin Bormann never resurfaced. Roger smuggled the bags home with him where they had remained undisturbed ever since.

"What did you do with the Bormann cases, Roger?" Skerritt had come across the Lance Corporal just after the German had vanished, but had caught sight of the tell-tale lettering on the briefcase and knew the importance of what was inside.

"They're both safe, and in a place where no-one but myself will find them. There have been more people than you looking for them over the years. Call them my insurance policy; once they're found, my life won't be worth much."

"And Madeline, how much does she know?"

"More than you do, and she took it to the grave with her. You can't touch her now."

In truth the lady in question was, at that very moment, standing on the other side of the door leading up the stairs and had heard every word of the conversation. They had long prepared for such a time as this, and she made her way silently along the corridor and down into the cellar to the concealed hiding place which Roger had constructed many years before.

"You know Roger; you have within your grasp a wealth of secret papers relating to the concealment of many senior Nazis who escaped justice after Nuremberg. Why not just let them go to the correct authorities?"

"How do I know that you are the 'correct authorities' Tom? Can I be sure that you aren't one of the old Fifth Column? I could hand them over, see you disappear and a few days later be faced with one of your assassination squads."

"You know that there are others on the way as we speak don't you? The 'Organisation' they call themselves. And they have connections at the highest level within the forces of law and order in the UK. I ran across a couple of them on the east coast, and they took down one of my associates for the sake of some photographs in his possession."

Skerritt was running out of options and they both knew it. Fretwell smiled across the room and was about to speak when a figure appeared, framed in the door casing. Julie Martin took in the scene before her very quickly as she stepped past her husband and into the room. Skerritt was stunned; he hadn't expected them to turn up here.

14

*T*here was an awkward silence for what seemed a very long time whilst Tom Skerritt and the Martins regarded each other with considerable suspicion. Julie was almost sure in her own mind that he had set up the break in at their caravan in an effort to obtain a copy of the letter, whilst he in his turn was beginning to wonder whether they had been working with Miranda and Gregory Farnley all along. Roger Fretwell broke the silence, sensing that neither party was actually a threat to him or Madeline after all.

"Why don't I put the kettle on, and we'll all have a nice cup of tea whilst you get a little better acquainted now that you're away from home." His sense of irony was one of the things which had attracted Madeline to him all those years ago,

Doug Martin was forced to smile at the man's sense of humour, and that one single statement reduced the tense atmosphere to something calmer in an instant. Julie turned her attention to the old man.

"You're Roger Fretwell aren't you? When we called earlier in the year it was to ask about the writer of a letter which I found amongst my aunt's possessions before she died."

"I am young lady. Ma and I did wonder about that visit, but she believed you were looking at buying the cottage further up the row. I knew she were wrong but when you women get something in your heads, its best not to argue."

"Who's 'Ma'?" cut in Skerritt suddenly.

"Second marriage, Tom. Couldn't bear being alone when Maddie went."

"What about Mr Skerritt, where does he fit into all of this?" Julie persisted.

"Well Tom and I go way back to our time in the army, and when the war ended I came home and he got involved in 'other things' shall we say. I have something that he wants but there are other people interested in acquiring it as well. I just can't make up my mind whether to trust any of them."

All the time this conversation was taking place, Skerritt had been sitting in a corner chair puffing away at his pipe, looking at those assembled for some sign of an opening. He now saw his chance. Taking a wallet from his inside pocket, he produced an official looking identification card bearing a crown and seal which Roger Fretwell had only seen once before in his life. That one had belonged to a senior member of the military police in Germany at the end of April 1945. He had been in command of an elite squad charged with rooting out any senior Nazis fleeing the country after the capitulation. The men under his command had told harrowing tales of places which the army NCO's in Roger's regiment had never heard of; the names bore testament to evil – Belsen, Auschwitz, Dachau and Treblinka.

"Wondered what happened to you after the war. I can see why you might be interested in the stuff I brought home, but it doesn't change my mind. That card could be a forgery for all I know and you'll need more proof before I even think of handing anything over."

"You should consider yourself lucky that I got to you first. If the Mossad knew what you've been hiding all these years you wouldn't be sitting comfortably here now. Look what they did with Adolf Eichmann and Klaus Barbie, do you really think that you would be safe in their hands?"

Fretwell had to admit that he had a point. There were paramilitary organisations at large which wouldn't think twice about the lengths that they would go to in order to retrieve the contents of Bormann's briefcases. Nevertheless he decided to hold out until he was surer of Skerritt and the people he represented. Julie had sat quietly during this conversation, but now interrupted with a question of her own.

"What exactly is in the briefcases Roger?" Fretwell smiled knowingly and looked across at Skerritt, who removed his pipe and turned to her.

"Inside those quite ordinary looking leather cases are sets of documents relating to a number of senior members of the Nazi Party, their families, any assets they held at the end of the conflict and new identities created for them inside this country. Some of these people occupy positions of considerable power and influence in government and industry There was a network inside the UK in 1946 which was geared up to the perpetuation of the Third Reich in the event of a defeat at the hands of the allies, and all that they need is the destruction of the papers and the elimination of anyone knowing of their existence. They are preparing for resurgence, and unless I can get my hands on the files first, they may succeed. All I need to do is convince Roger of my good intentions."

"And the Farnleys?"

"A sleeper cell set up by the same organisation to watch and wait. There are a number of them dotted around the country and I'm afraid that you stumbled across Miranda at just the wrong time for me. I can only imagine how she must have felt when you turned up on her doorstep asking about Madeline Colson. I knew of their existence of course, but not their names or where they were living. Now that they are out in the open their organisation will probably eliminate them and set up another cell from scratch; there are always people coming through the ranks and willing to take on that kind of work. They're terrorists."

"That's terrible." Doug interjected.

"That, Mr Martin, is why they are called terrorists." Skerritt couldn't resist the macabre joke, and it served to lighten the atmosphere which had pervaded the room.

It was almost certain that Miranda would have reported in to her control officer, and the organisation would now change its tactic from that of watching to actively seeking out those responsible for concealing the files they wanted. His phone rang – it was Bert Peterson and the man sounded quite agitated. He had narrowly missed a visit from two cars full of what looked like a hit squad at his home. Coming around the corner of the street on the way back from the local shops, he saw a number of men hurry up the front yard of his house. In minutes they were inside, and running across the street he knocked on the door of a neighbour's house and watched the activity from the woman's front window. The men came out a while later carrying several items, one of which was his laptop. The files from his camera were on the hard drive and it wouldn't take them long to find what they were probably looking for.

"You need to move quickly before they get down there." He told Skerritt. "I'm going to my daughter's for the time being, but they're bound to be with you by the end of tomorrow."

This was just what he needed. Handing the mobile to Fretwell, he let Bert tell the rest of the story of the activities on the east coast. At the end of the call Fretwell looked concerned and all the light-heartedness had vanished from his manner. Making an excuse to leave the room he went down to the cellar to put Madeline in the picture. Giving her Skerritt's mobile number he told her to go and stay with friends for a while and call him each day. He returned to the front room with an overnight bag packed with a few essentials.

"Ok, let's go." He was on his way out to Skerritt's car before the others had moved. Outside he turned to Julie. "It's more than likely my dear that your home will also receive a visit from Tom's 'friends'. Depending upon where your children are you can either come along with us and hide your car, or find somewhere else to stay for a while."

Julie looked at Doug. One phone call to his parents would take care of the children, and she was not about to back out of a mystery now that she was so close to discovering its roots.

"We're coming along. The car can stay here and we'll travel with you. Where exactly are we going?"

"Let me worry about that" Fretwell smiled "Tom can drive and I'll navigate; the less you know about our destination the better at present. Out of Tewkesbury and head north Mr Skerritt if you please, and I think you'd better put your foot down."

Needing very little in the way of encouragement now that he had gained Roger Fretwell's confidence, Skerritt moved off and they were soon clear of the town. With one phone call to update London on his situation, he followed Roger's instructions and headed for the M5 and a journey towards the Midlands.

15

*I*t had been fortunate for all those involved in the search that they had vacated their respective homes with such rapid efficiency. The property recovered from Bert Peterson's house was transferred to a secure location where it appeared, upon closer examination, to contain all the information which was needed to lead those in possession of it to the address in Tewkesbury. A black saloon car arrived at the cottages only a few hours after the departure of Skerritt's party, and one call to headquarters in London had elicited the registration number of Tom's car from the licensing authority in Swansea. With that information, an instruction was issued by the man at New Scotland Yard to all county police forces. They were to be on the lookout for a vehicle matching the description and registration of that belonging to Skerritt, but were to make no efforts to detain it.

The first report of the car heading north on the M5 motorway came in soon after. In minutes the black saloon was off in pursuit at top speed. It soon became clear to those inside it that, with regular reports from motorway police, they were gaining on their quarry which was now in the vicinity of Birmingham and heading for the M6. Their instructions were clear – retrieval of the files in the briefcases was of paramount importance and no witnesses should be left to complicate matters afterwards; the four travellers were to be eliminated.

Inside Skerritt's car, the conversation was also centred upon the consequences of finding the cases and their contents, and Roger Fretwell was under no illusion as to what was likely to happen if they were intercepted. Doug was beginning to doubt the wisdom of their coming along but Julie's mind was made up; they were seeing it through to the end. Skerritt's full tank of petrol meant that there would be no need for any stops on the motorway, and this was the one fact which had worked in their favour, as the pursuing vehicle was compelled to make one refuelling call along the way.

"Alright, where is it exactly that we're going?" Julie resurrected the question which had first been posed at the cottage.

"Morecambe" Roger replied "Maddie and I bought a place there in the fifties with the money from the sale of dad's garage business. We used it for holidays whilst the children were growing up and let it out during the rest of the summer."

"So the cases are hidden there?"

"Yes my dear, at the back of a concealed partition which I built many years ago. Madeline and I are the only ones who know its position. You would never find it on your own."

"Madeline, present tense? You said she was dead at the cottage." Skerritt cast a reproving glance to one side at Roger.

"I did, but that was before I knew of your true intentions. She will, by now, be safely away from Tewkesbury and any danger at a place which we had decided upon should anything like this ever happen."

"When we get there, what then?" Julie had the bit between her teeth now "What are you going to do with the documents?"

"That rather depends upon Mr Skerritt and the people issuing his orders. If I am wrong and they get their hands on the documents, they will kill us all. If I am right and the people who are undoubtedly pursuing us arrive before there is time to retrieve the cases, then Tom's bosses will have set up a trap to apprehend the likes of the Farnleys when they turn up. Either way we are pawns in a game of high stakes and serious consequences."

Skerritt sighed. There was now no way of concealing his plans any further, and in any case they were far too close to the end game for it to matter anyway.

"This car carries a surveillance device which has been relaying all of our conversations back to an office in London. The people I work for have known of our general direction since we left the cottages, and are now aware that we are on our way to the North West. Preparations will have been made to set up a welcoming party just outside the town and they will accompany us to our destination. When our followers show up, they will be dealt with quickly and efficiently leaving me to return the cases to those who know what to do with them. With any luck the organisation concealing the Neo-Nazi organisation will be identified and wound down within a month."

"What about us?" Doug asked "How safe are we with you?"

"As safe as we are ourselves, Mr Martin. You and your wife have put yourselves in considerable danger, and your efforts will be suitably rewarded once the matter is over. However once we arrive at Roger's property, and just in case my associates are not already there, I suggest that you conceal yourselves in the event that something goes wrong. That way you will still have the car as a means of escape, and my organisation will be able to track your route."

The rest of the trip up to the holiday resort passed without incident, but all of Skerritt's instincts told him that he was still not home and dry as far as Roger Fretwell was concerned. That he had gained the man's confidence was not in doubt, but something told him that the individual at the side of him had an agenda all of his own as far as the documents in the briefcases were concerned, and that this would not become apparent until all of his own cards were on the table. He shot a sideways glance at the man, and checking that the Martins were asleep ventured to tease information from him.

"You've read the files I assume?"

"Many times, and they make quite a splendid tale; a real set of ripping yarns if they're true."

"If?"

"Why not? There have been many attempts to destabilise the government in this country since the war, just look at what nearly happened to Harold Wilson's in the sixties. Why shouldn't this be just one more?"

"Meaning what?"

"Meaning that the files could really be authentic, but the fuss over who has them could really be nothing more than a blind to create confusion and distrust at the highest levels within government and the forces of law and order. Look Tom, once any organisation got

71

their hands on those documents God only knows what they could be made to say."

"That would be treason. No one in their right mind would undertake such a devastating operation."

"Alright, let me ask you this. How much do you actually trust those who set you on this track? How long have you been waiting for some clue as to my whereabouts? How fortunate was it that you bumped into these two at the library in Cleethorpes? Couldn't it all have been set up to draw you out and into the chase?"

Skerritt had not even begun to consider that he may be some kind of sacrificial lamb - a bait to draw out something or someone of far greater consequence. Yes the files could prove a devastating blow to establishment figures, but he had always taken it on trust that he was actually working for the right side. It was true that he had never actually met any of those with whom he had been in constant contact over the years, but that was not unusual in the circumstances. A small seed of nagging doubt was now germinating at the back of his mind as they entered the outskirts of the town.

"Take the coast road; you'll know the way back in case we have to make a run for it. In a couple of miles there's a right hand turn up a farm track, and the cottage is at the end. It's partially concealed behind a stand of poplars, but there's a good view of the lower part of the road, so we'll see anyone coming a mile off."

The property was a whitewashed two storey holiday cottage facing the sea, and the closed shutters told Skerritt that it was currently unoccupied. The Martins awoke as the car pulled up behind the building and the three occupants of the vehicle followed Fretwell to the front door as he produced a key ring from his pocket. The shuttered rooms were very dark, and with the car now concealed from immediate view nothing was done to attract any attention to their visit. Roger led the way upstairs to the bathroom, where he carefully removed a well-concealed panel from behind the toilet cistern. From the small space he pulled a parcel bound in Hessian cloth which revealed, once opened, two faded brown briefcases wrapped in oilcloth. The three of them held their collective breath as Roger opened the bundle up. There, on the leather front strap of one of the cases, was the faded but still discernible gold embossed lettering 'M. B.'

Returning to the lower rooms, Fretwell placed the cases on the table in front of Tom Skerritt and waited. Doug and Julie had expected some feverish opening of the long-hidden baggage, but Tom Skerritt just smiled. He had been looking for these things for over forty years, and now that they were out in the open and in front of him, he was not sure how to react. Roger Fretwell broke the spell.

"Ok, now I believe you Skerritt. I wasn't sure which side you were on until just then. I half expected a bullet after I brought the cases out, but it wouldn't have done you any good; take a look inside."

Tom Skerritt, along with Doug and Julie, frowned in puzzlement. Opening first one, then the other of the cases almost reverently, it was Julie who stepped back in astonishment.

"They're gone! There's nothing in there."

"There never was young lady, at least not here. I knew that someone would come looking for the documents once I'd read them and realised what they meant. The files are safe and sound with Madeline and I'm the only person who knows where she is."

He turned to Tom Skerritt, now standing with a broad smile upon his face. He would have done exactly the same in Roger's position. The man had no guarantee of coming out of this alive once the papers had been given up. Their attention was drawn to the doorway, where a tall, distinguished looking man in his fifties was standing. He stepped into the room and said one word.

"Fostropp"

16

Skerritt stepped forward and introduced the rest of the assembled group to the man to whom he had made his initial report after Julie's trip to the library. Following on from these preliminaries and after a brief silence during which the stranger subjected each of them to a visual examination, he spoke again.

"My name, as far as you are concerned is George Watkinson. Whether or not you believe that to be true is of no importance right now. We have arranged a delay for your pursers just south of Galgate on the M6, but I suggest that we leave immediately as they will almost certainly have summoned reinforcements from Lancaster where they have a base in this area. I assume that the documents are not in either of the cases, that would have been too easy and I have to admit, something of a disappointment. The Martins will travel with me, and we will follow you, Skerritt back to wherever in the Tewkesbury area the files are really located."

George Watkinson occupied an influential position within the corridors of power at the centre of government in London. His responsibilities within the security services gave him the ability to move in and out of the various departments which are responsible for ensuring that the nation's defences operate effectively at all times. He reported to no-one but the Cabinet Office and the Prime Minister, and if questioned about him it is highly unlikely that the vast majority of the MPs at Westminster would even be aware of his existence. He was a man of impeccable standards and demanded no less of those who reported to him. His manner could be charming at the utmost when required, but he was not someone with whom you would like to cross swords.

He had been aware for some years of a covert organisation within the UK which was committed to the establishment of a Fascist state in Britain, and had worked tirelessly to ensure that it did not happen. However, each time his operatives had come close to breaking into the net which held it together, those under the microscope had simply faded from the picture. That there was a mole somewhere within the department was beyond doubt, but try as he may there had been no success to date in exposing him or her. The Farnleys were just the latest cell to be removed before he could get to them.

As he stared out of the tinted windows of the black Mercedes now speeding back down the M6, he pondered the current situation. He was vulnerable whilst out of his comfort zone in the capital. There, he was surrounded by a team of staff committed to his cause, and safe within his power base was almost untouchable. Out here in the wilds of Britain he was at the mercy of each and every county police force which could be mobilised against him. Those whom he sought had operatives in key positions within the Metropolitan Police and every major city force. Should his whereabouts become known, arrest would be almost immediate and his position of secrecy compromised. None in government would dare to admit to his position and he would be hung out to dry. It was a situation which he accepted with some pragmatism – it went with the territory.

The Martins had remained silent for some time, and whilst Doug was quite happy with that situation, his wife was not one to let an opportunity go begging, and her innate curiosity began to get the better of her.

"What happens if we run into any of the people who have been following us, Mr Watkinson?"

Putting away the newspaper which he had been scrutinising, Watkinson removed his spectacles and put them in his top pocket. The Martins already knew too much to risk alienating them and he wasn't in the business of disposing of innocent bystanders, particularly when they had been instrumental in exposing both the location of Roger Fretwell, and also the existence of the East Coast cell which had hitherto remained concealed. He smiled across the limousine and clasped his hands across his lap like some benevolent

75

headmaster at a prize giving ceremony. His voice though, was one of hardened steel.

"There are other vehicles in our little convoy, Mrs Martin, whose job it is to keep a lookout for a tail. They are highly skilled in concealment and close by at all times. No, no, it is of very little use you looking out of the windows for them; we never advertise our presence to the general motorist, but it is likely that our pursuers will try to flush us out of hiding at some point before we reach London. It just remains to be seen what tactics they will use. Should they achieve the unlikely circumstance of detaining us for whatever reason, we will all be arrested on a trumped up charge and taken to some regional headquarters. From there they will attempt to make us disappear, but fear not dear lady this car is bullet proof and the windows will take a direct shot from most firearms. You are quite safe as long as you remain with me."

"What about Roger and Mr Skerritt?"

"That is a different matter. From our opponents' point of view they must be allowed to proceed unhindered to their final destination, otherwise the files remain concealed. Should that happen, the documents will inevitably re-emerge at some future time and the whole process would begin again. No, this is their opportunity to capture and destroy the evidence once and for all and they will go to extraordinary lengths to achieve that end. My main concern is that we do not become separated from them, but Mr Skerritt knows exactly what to do in that eventuality"

The Mercedes was travelling in the centre lane and approaching junction 31A for Fulwood when the driver brought Watkinson's attention to a 'boxing' manoeuvre by three approaching vehicles. This was clearly an attempt to force them to leave at the next intersection and an event for which they had all been prepared. A brief radio call brought two large box vans and a container lorry alongside to block off the slip road in the nearside lane. Once past the junction, the convoy vehicles saw to it that the offending traffic was itself forced away on to the hard shoulder and carefully pushed down a gentle grass bank and away from the road. With a clear path now before them, Watkinson's party sped on south of Preston towards the link with the M61, but he was certain that this was not the last they would see of any pursuing vehicles.

They caught up with Skerritt's car as they skirted Manchester on the

M60, heading across the Pennines on the A57 Snake Pass for an intersection with the M1 at Sheffield. The roads across the hills were too narrow for the sort of tactics used on the M6 and any following vehicles would be clearly visible, so a stop was made at the Cat and Fiddle whilst all parties in the convoy reassembled. While Watkinson briefed the drivers, Julie took the opportunity to take Roger Fretwell to one side.

"I've not had the chance until now, but I think this should be returned to you." She handed him the letter which had set her off on the search in the first place.

He smiled as he read the contents again for the first time since he had originally written to Madeline all those years ago. Turning the small cardboard ticket over in his fingers, he shook his head as the memories of that day came flooding back.

"I originally thought that she had ignored this, and I sat sulking for a month or so. Mother wasn't convinced and told me to write again. It was all history after that. You say your aunt picked it up? I must have dropped it on the way to the post office with some other items of mail. Thank you for returning it, Madeline will be so pleased to see it, I'm sure."

Their brief conversation was interrupted by George Watkinson, who beckoned Fretwell to one side where Skerritt was already standing.

"I think we need to make some arrangements for the recovery of the papers. I understand from Tom here that your wife knows where they are and that she is currently staying with friends. Can you tell me where that would be?"

"In truth Mr Watkinson I don't know. We have an arrangement designed to cover a situation just like this. She would leave the cottage and go to a predetermined location which she kept secret even from me, and I had something similar for the same reason. Until she contacts me on Tom's mobile, and she is due right about now, I have no idea what she is doing."

"When she does call you it is important that we arrange to have her collected and transported to London without delay. Out on her own, and with the location of those documents known only to her, she is at risk."

As if on cue, Skerritt's mobile rang and he handed it to Fretwell.

"Maddie dear, listen carefully I have some instructions for you. We are quite safe and there will be a car coming to pick you up as soon as we know where you are. Right, so you'll be at Monica's for the rest of today. Look, don't go back to the hideaway; Mr Watkinson says that his colleagues will come for you. What? Just a moment." He turned to Watkinson "She says how will your man identify himself. Right. Maddie, he will say just one word to you, and if he doesn't use that word you are to stay where you are and ring the police – the word is 'Fostropp'. Yes dear 'Fostropp', and you can go with him."

A sudden burst of activity amongst the drivers had everyone getting back into their respective vehicles as Watkinson reported an advance sighting of three cars by their 'tail end Charlie' a few miles back. Once back on the motorway system it would be easier to avoid contact, but out here on the moor land it was possible that an ambush could be sprung. Watkinson called ahead to arrange company for the chasing pack of vehicles, which would find the road before them inexplicably blocked by farm equipment which appeared to have suddenly broken down. Issuing instructions to the other drivers in their group, he changed the route and headed south from Sheffield on the A621 for Chesterfield and the M1 at junction 29. Any intercepting party further north would now be wrong-footed, giving them a head start on the two hundred mile trip back to the capital and safety. If he thought that they were out of the woods however, he was to be unpleasantly surprised.

17

*A*lan Mason's orders to his operatives had been quite clear. They were to recover the documents from Roger Fretwell by any means necessary and at all costs. Perhaps he should have made it clear in words of one syllable that under no circumstances was anyone to be allowed to evade capture. The squad he had sent to Tewkesbury had missed all of them by a matter of hours and had failed to prevent them reaching their destination. Despite backup from the North West they had still contrived to allow their quarry to escape across the Pennines and were now blocked at both ends of a country road by a couple of tractors. The carefully planned interception on the motorway had been foiled and the local police had failed to turn up in time to rectify the situation. Now away from the M1, Fretwell and his associates were out of Mason's control and presumably heading south by some other route. He punched a number into his mobile phone.

"Collins, you followed the woman from the cottage didn't you? Ok, so we know where she is. I want you over there immediately to pick her up and make sure that you're convincing. I don't know, get a police uniform man; do I have to think of everything?"

He cursed at the incompetence of the batch of recruits which were coming through at the moment; why did he seem to get all the brainless ones? Madeline Colson was his last card. With her in his hands Fretwell would have no alternative than to hand over whatever files he had been hiding for the past forty-five years. He got up from his desk and donned his coat, it was time for an update report and thirty minutes later saw him entering the hallway of the Cabinet Office in Whitehall. The man he was about to see occupied one of the prime positions of power in the government and he was not looking forward to the dressing down he would receive as a result of the fiasco of the last couple of days.

With ears still ringing an hour and a half later, Mason emerged from the Whitehall office in no doubt as to the lengths he would now have to go in order to satisfy those in whose hands his future rested. Nothing less than retrieval of the files and an elimination of all those who had seen them would suffice. An update call to Collins to pass on the kicking he had received set in motion a scaled-up version of the plan he had outlined to the man earlier. This was now a shoot to kill policy.

The dark blue Sierra pulled up outside the address in Gloucester which had been given by George Watkinson. A smartly dressed young man stepped out of the front passenger seat, straightened his tie and walked up the path to the house and rang the bell. He smiled as Madeline opened the door and gave the single word identification which she had been expecting. Moments later she was in the back seat and the car pulled away heading east along the A40 towards Cheltenham.

Collins turned up at the address as the vehicle was leaving and radioed in to Mason that he was in pursuit. Turning the BMW motorbike around, he followed them at a discreet distance past Churchtown and into open countryside. Here he made his move, overtaking the car and waving the driver to pull in. Watkinson had instructed his team to keep a low profile and not attract the attention of the local police, and the driver cursed his luck as he eased the saloon into a lay-by and stopped. The traffic cop kicked the side stand down, pulled the BWM to a 'rest' position and slowly removed his gloves, placing them into one of the panniers from which he drew a firearm. He approached the Sierra from a distance of around ten yards and with his visor still down. Identification would be impossible and with the driver already winding down the side window, the rest of the job was going to be easy.

Raising the silenced gun at the last moment, he fired three shots through the open window and all the occupants slumped and were still. Checking for any approaching traffic he searched the car from back to front for the papers which Mason had told him would be there, but found nothing. The man would not be pleased, and with time moving on and the chance of being spotted increasing with each moment of delay, he returned to the bike, kick started it and sped off. The debriefing would not be pleasant but as a mere operative following instructions any repercussions would be unlikely to filter down to his level. The important thing now was to ditch the uniform and bike and get to the pre-arranged rendezvous point as soon as possible.

The journey to the 'dead letter box' used by Madeline Colson in Cheltenham was a short one, and Watkinson had expected a call from his team within an hour of their departure from Gloucester. When that did not happen he knew that something was wrong and sent out another car to shadow the journey. They arrived at the scene to find local emergency services already there and two ambulances leaving the site of the shooting at high speed. Local police flagged them down along with other motorists to ask if any of them had seen or heard anything but they managed to follow the departing emergency vehicles to their destination. Watkinson's response to the update was unequivocal.

"Get to the A&E and find out what's happening. Don't let the three of them out of your sight for an instant. If anybody gets in your way, tell them it's a matter of national security and show them your ID cards. I'll make sure that you get some back up within the hour, and I'll be with you as soon as I can."

His next job was more complicated. Flashing Skerritt to pull over, Watkinson told the two of them that there had been an accident on the way to Cheltenham and that Madeline had been taken to a local hospital. He mentioned nothing about the shooting for fear of upsetting the plans for retrieving the documents. The order of the convoy now changed, and with emergency sirens and lights now showing a swathe was cut through the busy motorway traffic as they headed South West.

In Skerritt's car, Roger was thunderstruck. He didn't believe the story about an accident for a moment but there was nothing that he could do but go along with Watkinson for the moment. He had no idea where Madeline had been going, since the hiding place of the files was known only to her and this was another precautionary tactic which they had decided upon some years ago. If she were now dead he would have lost the only woman he had ever loved, and the information which she had been protecting could be gone forever. The journey to Cheltenham passed without further incident and seemed to take an age. Arriving at the accident and emergency department they were all directed to a small waiting room where a member of the surgical staff met them.

"I am Simon Wathall, surgical consultant. Are any of you related to the three casualties?"

"George Watkinson, MI5. The two men work for me, but the woman is the wife of Roger Fretwell here."

"I see. Mr Fretwell your wife is stable and out of immediate danger for the moment, but one of the bullets lodged against her spine and we won't know until she regains consciousness whether there will be any permanent damage."

"Bullets? What happened, we were told that there had been an accident; there was no mention of any guns." He looked at Watkinson for clarification. They all sat down.

"Roger, my information was that they had been intercepted and shot by someone posing as a police officer. My men found a BWM motorbike and discarded clothing dumped at the side of the road some five miles from the scene of the shooting. Someone clearly thought that Madeline had the files with her when she obviously did not. I'm sorry to be insensitive, but as soon as she comes round we need to find out where they are hidden."

He turned back to the consultant and asked after the condition of his men, but the look on the man's face said it all. They had, he went on to elaborate, sustained fatal head injuries from gunshot wounds from a nine millimetre hand gun and had been pronounced dead on arrival at the hospital. The bodies would be sent to the mortuary for autopsy and information would be released to MI5 as soon as it was over. For the moment there was nothing that any of them could do apart from wait until Madeline was able to speak; until that happened a twenty-four hour armed guard was placed upon the room where she lay, and no-one except Roger was allowed near her without Watkinson's express permission.

18

*R*oger had kept a constant vigil at Madeline's bedside as she slipped in and out of consciousness while the medical staff carried out a series of tests to determine her level of fitness for surgery. The bullet lodged dangerously close to her spine would have to come out, but at the age of seventy it was by no means certain that she would survive the operation. They had talked, very quietly and privately during her moments of clarity, and Roger had maintained a stoical manner throughout. He slept when she slept, always with her hand in his, so that at the slightest movement he would be awake and attentive to her needs. She was in a great deal of pain and concealed it well from everyone apart from her husband, but it was becoming clear that the removal of the bullet would have to be sooner rather than later to save her from being paralyzed for life. After a long discussion, the two of them agreed that an operation to extract it should go ahead without delay. She was prepped for theatre during the evening and Roger retired to a small but comfortable side room to await the outcome.

Tom Skerritt had returned to his home in Cleethorpes, promising to keep in touch but George Watkinson had been an almost constant visitor. This was not entirely an altruistic gesture; he was also concerned at the level of security in the hospital and the ability of his men to protect the Fretwells from attack. He was with Roger when the surgeon sought them out in the early hours of the morning. The man was exhausted after eight hours of a delicate and difficult operation and spoke very quietly to them both. Roger slumped back into his seat from the standing position he had adopted when seeing the man approach. With head in hands his body heaved in a torrent of tears as Watkinson sat beside him, one arm around his shoulders. The surgeon left, there was nothing more that he could do now.

The news that the final victim in the Cheltenham shooting had succumbed to her injuries was released to the press the next morning, and Watkinson made arrangements for Madeline's coffin to be transported the short journey back to Tewkesbury. With Roger in no fit state to take any part in the funeral arrangements, it fell to his eldest son, Brian, to step into the breach. He had travelled down from Newcastle with his wife earlier in the week, and they had stayed at the cottage. A short service was conducted at the same church which the Martins had used for Molly, and the packed congregation moved on to the crematorium en masse for the final tributes.

Two weeks later, and with all relatives now returned to their homes in various parts of the country, Roger sat alone in the sitting room of the cottage where he and Madeline had spent so many happy hours. He snapped out of the trance into which he had fallen almost an hour ago and picked up the newspaper. Stepping out into the warm late afternoon sunshine, he made his way down to the river bank and sat on the bench where they both liked to watch the summer sunsets. Neighbours had kept a watchful eye upon him since the departure of family, and Albert from next door now strolled across the green to join Roger. They sat in silence for some while as long-time neighbours are apt to do, but after struggling for an opening line for a while Albert tested the water.

"Lovely evening coming, eh Roger?"

"What? Oh yes, I suppose so. I hadn't really noticed to tell the truth."

"Aye, well that's not really surprising in the circumstances. How've you been these last few days?"

"Hmmm? Oh, keeping busy you know. There's the garden to keep going, and I've got the cat for company. Maddie would have loved this."

He stared out across the broadening river as it meandered towards it's confluence with the Severn and remembered their children growing up and playing on the banks of the Avon. The ducks and other wildfowl returned each year and the entire scene was one of peace and tranquillity in an otherwise frenetic world. He sighed and stood up, the newspaper falling from his lap as he turned to return to the cottage. Albert picked it up and gave it back to him, pointing towards the small car park at the end of the row.

"Looks like company, you been expecting anybody?"

Roger shook his head as George Watkinson stepped out of the anonymous light blue Vauxhall Astra. He was dressed in casuals and came down to the river to meet him half way as Albert went back to his own home.

"Nice to see you again. Mr Watkinson."

"George" He corrected as they shook hands.

"George then. Come inside and we'll have a cup of tea shall we?"

Now inside the cottage and out of the public gaze, the mood lightened considerably as Roger's face broke into a smile which he hadn't used for quite a while.

"How is she?"

"Much better" replied Watkinson as he sat down "The bullet was as close as the surgeon had indicated but she was never in the kind of danger which we put out to the press. We managed to keep her under wraps once out of the hospital and all records of her stay there have been removed to a safer place."

"When will she be able to come home?"

"Home?" Watkinson frowned "Certainly not here. The funeral and cremation were all too public for that to happen. We might have to provide new identities for the both of you, and I suggest that you seriously consider moving well away from this area at least until we have the chance to recover the files and eliminate any threat to the two of you. What about that place up in Morecambe? Is there anyone up there who knows who you are?"

"Not really. It was more of a holiday cottage than anything else. We should be able to get by without too much trouble. Will we ever be able to come back here?"

"Maybe, but not for a while, and then there'll be some explaining to do."

Madeline's 'death' had been part of a carefully contrived plan to take the heat out of the situation and give Watkinson and his staff the time to find the papers which they were all so desperately seeking.

She was the only one who knew the exact location of the bundle of documents, and had now revealed that secret to the head of MI5. He had decided to let them lie there for a while longer in order to draw out any further attempts to extract the information from Roger, and it was now imperative that both he and Madeline make their separate ways out of the county for the foreseeable future.

As far as George's sources could tell him, there had been little or no activity from those responsible for the deaths of his agents, and the assassin himself was still at large. Curiously, they had managed to find one witness who got a very good look at a policeman apparently changing his clothes in a lane off the A40. This man left the uniform and the bike where it had been later found, and boarded a bus heading in the opposite direction for Gloucester. That journey would have taken him back past the site of the shooting and allowed him the chance to reassess the situation. He showed Roger a photo fit likeness which had been made up from the description, but shaking his head he told Watkinson that he had never seen the man before. Sadly neither had Madeline, but MI5 had been faced with this kind of situation before – the man could run, but he would not be able to hide forever.

"What happened to the Farnley's? Tom Skerritt told me about them."

"Vanished completely. Their house is up for sale, and we suspect that their organisation will have dealt with them in some way so that they won't cause any more embarrassment."

An hour later, the decision had been made. Roger would put the cottage up for sale, telling all those local to him that he could no longer stand to live there without his wife. There would, of course, be an outpouring of sympathy but no-one would be told of his destination and two weeks later following a quick sale of the property, neighbours were waving goodbye as the removal van pulled away from the little backwater and its row of chocolate box cottages. As they rounded the final corner, Roger took one look backwards and wondered if he would ever set eyes on the place again.

19

*T*hough she had survived the operation to remove the bullet from near her spine, Madeline's recovery had been neither a speedy nor an easy one. At seventy years of age she and Roger had always kept themselves fit and healthy, and although they were both aware of the dangers surrounding the papers he brought back from Germany after the war, neither had been prepared for the ferocity of the attack by Alan Mason's gunman. A few inches higher and the wound would certainly have been fatal and Madeline was fortunate to be sitting in the rear seats of the car at the time George Watkinson's men had been shot and killed.

The ruse of getting her out of the hospital and away to a safe house had been facilitated by the death of an old woman in an adjacent ward. Watkinson had wielded his immense power and influence over the hospital staff to get the two women swapped over during one night of the week following Madeline's operation, and the paperwork was completed under the controls of the Official Secrets Act which the head of MI5 had insisted the surgeon sign. From that point on the body of the unknown woman became that of Madeline, and the process of returning her to Tewkesbury for the funeral moved swiftly and without a hitch. Madeline herself was currently living under armed guard in a flat in Finchley where she had provided Watkinson with details of the hiding place of the files he sought.

She had, after the war, given up full time nursing in favour of making a home for herself and Roger in the South West. One of her hobbies had been books and reading, and when a part-time vacancy appeared at the local library she took up the post of assistant to the librarian. She left there in 1949 for a similar position in Cheltenham and took responsibility for the library's archives. This was where she decided to conceal the 'Bormann' papers as her husband called them. Wrapped in the same waxed brown paper as the rest of the material there and tied with identical sisal twine, she had coded the outer wrapper to match in with the other numerous bundles in the dusty storeroom on the top floor. Known only to her, the exact position of the files would be safe from discovery until such time as they would be needed. Now that time had come.

She gave George Watkinson precise details as to where the documents were located, and he made the trip to the Central Library in Cheltenham personally to retrieve the bundle. Posing as a government official from the central land registry, his carefully prepared credentials gained him almost immediate access to the archive store room indicated by Madeline. The staff almost fell over themselves to be helpful, and it was only after accepting repeated offers for tea that he was eventually left alone.

The place was musty, with that distinct but not unpleasant aroma of an old-fashioned front parlour which families only tended to use on special occasions, and which had not seen the lighting of a fire for months. It reminded him of one of the bedrooms where his three maiden aunts had lived in the fifties. They too had used it as a 'box' room and he stood momentarily as memories of those years came back to him. Smiling and shaking his head at his own whimsicality, he started to work at finding the long-lost papers. He quickly mastered the logic of the filing system and its logging methodology, and unfolding a set of step ladders climbed to the top shelf of the central section. He ran his finger along the labels on each package, removing a thick film of dust in the process, and had to move several stacks of parcels before he came across the identification number he was seeking. This of course was not the bundle he required; that was positioned three stacks to the right and was the bottom parcel in the column. Madeline had written these details in order that anyone intercepting him would de misdirected to the wrong set of papers – only George knew the actual place to look.

Replacing the rest of the material back into its original position, he took the parcel to the table at the end of the room and switched on the overhead light. A sudden noise and movement from behind at the door startled him, and he dropped his coat neatly over the package.

"Found what you need?" It was the head librarian Ben Groves, keen to make a favourable impression on the 'Man from the Ministry' as his staff had referred to Watkinson.

"Not quite yet, but I'm sure I'll be alright. There's no need to bother yourself about me, I'm in my element in places like this."

"Ok, well if there's anything you do need, just give us a shout." He smiled and closed the door after one more look around the room.

Watkinson heaved a sigh of relief. A few moments later and the papers would have been laid out on the table for all to see; it would then have been extremely difficult to explain what he was doing in possession of old documents from Hitler's Third Reich. Nevertheless, he couldn't resist leafing through the old papers, and replacing them with a similar quantity of modern A4 sheets, he rewrapped the bundle exactly as he had first found it. Sitting down at the table and putting on a pair of cotton gloves, he leafed through the uppermost pages. They were all headed with the Imperial German Eagle, and each set carried the chilling title:

Geheime Staatspolizei

Strenges Geheimnis

Watkinson knew from his contacts with other European security agencies that the translation was 'Top Secret' and as he read through the first few sets, the devastating effect of the information contained within them began to dawn upon him. His department had always been led to believe that the contents of the 'dossiers' would expose a network of hidden Nazi party members within post-war British society, but he had no idea that the effect of any disclosure would go to the very heights of power in modern Britain. Emitting an involuntary low whistle he closed the fourth set of papers and placed the entire bundle into the false bottom of his briefcase, carefully spread so as not to arouse suspicion if searched.

Calling at the main desk on the library's ground floor, he placed his coat and briefcase alongside a chair at one of the reading tables close to a man engrossed in research of some kind. Once the formalities of announcing his departure had been completed, the head librarian returned to the store room to lock the door. Watkinson then collected his coat and picked up the briefcase from the opposite side of the researcher's chair and strolled out of the building via its main entrance. At no time were any words exchanged by the two of them, and neither one so much as glanced at the other. Once outside the library, George turned right and started to make his way back to the car he had left in one of the council car parks.

Tom Skerritt looked over the top of his glasses as George Watkinson went through the double doors at the end of the room. Moving the exchanged briefcase under the table, he carried on with his reading for five or ten more minutes before packing up his notes and neatly stacking the books he had been using in the centre of the table. George had provided him with an identical briefcase to his own in anticipation of some attempt to recover the papers, and his instructions were to vacate the premises and make his way to a pre-arranged meeting place to hand the bag over that afternoon. Picking up his coat and notebooks, he smiled at the librarian as he made for the side entrance to the building and the same car park which was the destination of Watkinson himself.

George had reached the corner of the street when two men dressed in casuals approached him from the other side of the road.

"Mr George Watkinson?" The taller of the two addressed him in an official yet surly manner.

"Who wants to know?" The reply was suitably official.

Warrant cards were produced identifying both men as officers with the local CID, and George scrutinised them carefully. He was extremely proficient in detecting forged documents of this nature and took his time with the current examination. The cards appeared to be genuine and he handed them back to the officers.

"Alright then, what's this all about?"

"You're to come along with us please sir."

"Do you have a warrant? Am I to understand that you are arresting me?"

"No we don't sir and no you are not, but it would be appreciated if you would get in the car and we could continue this conversation down at the station."

An unmarked car pulled up at the kerb alongside the three of them, and George briefly considered the prospect of refusing and simply walking away. This however, would draw attention to all of them and his position as head of MI5 was not one which welcomed publicity in any form. He nodded and stepped into the vehicle still wondering why the local police had been involved in what he regarded as an attempt to relieve him of the files which he no longer possessed. As the car pulled away, he glanced out at the figure of Tom Skerritt as he stood a little further down the street. An almost indistinguishable shake of the head as the vehicle passed him was enough to warn Skerritt that things had taken a not unexpected turn, and that the alternative plan which they had devised was now to come into operation. He pulled out a notebook from his inside coat pocket and read the address which Watkinson had given to him in anticipation of what had just occurred.

Pausing only to reassure himself that there was no likelihood of being followed, he walked briskly back to his car and set off for the house in question. The village of Bishop's Cleeve lies some two to three miles due north of Cheltenham and the place of his destination was a house on Evesham Road at the northern edge of the settlement. The area was quiet, particularly in the middle of the afternoon and he parked his car at the rear of the premises out of sight of the main road. Entering the property through the back door with a key given to him by Watkinson, he called a secure number from his mobile and sat down to await the arrival of those charged with the security of the briefcase which he had brought from the library.

20

*I*t had been mid afternoon at around two thirty when George Watkinson was intercepted outside the library in Cheltenham, and the journey to police headquarters had taken about fifteen minutes. It was now four o'clock, and apart from being booked in with the desk sergeant, he had been left alone in one of the interview rooms for a period in excess of an hour. The room itself was small with the customary table and four chairs (two for them and one each for you and your legal representative), and a large mirror to one side. He assumed that this was for observation purposes and his years of experience in such tactics had taught him to simply ignore it. His daily newspaper was on the table before him, crossword completed and read from cover to cover.

No-one had made any attempt to remove the brief case from his possession, and apart from a WPC bringing him tea at half hourly intervals he had seen no-one of any rank within the force. He sat back down at the table after a cursory walk around the room, put his feet up on the surface and closed his eyes. That would give them something to think about – he had studied all forms of relaxation techniques in his time and knew that there was nothing guaranteed to infuriate an interrogator more than a show of nonchalance. It must have worked, as there was the sound of activity in the corridor outside the door and what he assumed to be two detectives entered the room. Watkinson sat up, clasped his hands in front of himself and placed them carefully on the table top before him.

Of the two men on the other side of the table the first was scruffily dressed with his shirt unbuttoned and a tie, which appeared to still bear the marks of breakfast, skewed to one side. He was unshaven and surly looking, and lit a cigarette before looking around for an ashtray. The second, younger man was more neatly presented but still bore the same blank and uncompromising expression of his partner. They both made a show of going through a file of papers which they had brought along, and which Watkinson was unable to see as the manila folders were tilted away from him. Stubbing out his cigarette in the ashtray, the first detective cleared his throat, looked up into Watkinson's face and spoke.

"Right. Watkinson, George Watkinson, that's right isn't it?"

"My name is George Watkinson; you are correct." A statement delivered in a cool, calm and clear voice. The detective frowned – it had unnerved him.

"Been to the library have you?"

George was sorely tempted to make some trite remark about his books being overdue and not wanting to get into any trouble over it. He thought better and suppressed an overwhelming urge to reduce the interview to a farce. He wanted to know how far they were prepared to push the situation, and humour did not seem to be the best way of achieving that. He doubted whether either of them would recognise a joke if it jumped up and bit them.

"I have, yes that's true. Can you tell me what I have done wrong since I appear to have been arrested?"

"We'll ask the questions Mr Watkinson." A nettled and curt response – he had rattled them. "What was the reason for your visit there?"

They had certainly been set up with a stock list of questions and the real interrogator was probably observing from behind what was clearly a two-way mirror. He paused just long enough in his response to elicit a raised glance by both men from the papers which they had been scrutinising. These files would have absolutely nothing to do with the questions which they were asking, and had been brought along simply for effect.

"Research" A true statement as far as it went, and George intended to stick to fact wherever he could; there was less chance of being caught out that way, and in any case he had a prepared scenario for just such an occasion as this.

The first detective looked up again, his glance having returned to the manila folder. His attention span must be very short thought Watkinson – he was becoming bored already. Turning the tables on this pair would be quite easy.

"Research? What kind of research?" Wonderful, thought Watkinson, playing right into my hands.

The following half hour was taken up entirely by George Watkinson explaining in great detail about the science of genealogy and his lifelong interest in tracking down his family roots. He produced, from his briefcase, sheaves of papers detailing years of ploughing through parish and civil records obtained from a variety of establishments up and down the country. Each time the detectives tried to haul him back to their track he shot off on another tangent. His intention of appearing to be a complete anorak on the subject was working very nicely. Eventually, and out of sheer boredom, he cut them a break and drifted back to their version of reality but it was a very tired voice which got him there.

"So, let me get this straight, you went to the central library for no other reason than to dig around in some dusty old records for stuff about your family."

"Got it in one sergeant."

"Inspector!" A correction spat out with ill concealed irritation.

"My sincere apologies, Inspector"

"So why then, did you tell the library staff that you were from the ministry?"

"Because, inspector, I am willing enough to use my rank to gain access to a private room wherever possible. A place where I can sit in silence and concentrate on the job at hand without constant interruption."

"Rank? What rank would that be?" A sudden look of apprehension crossed the man's face. He obviously had no idea with whom he was talking, and Watkinson side-stepped the question for the moment with a few of his own.

"Why have I been brought here Inspector? What offence have I committed? You see I was always under the impression that this was the kind of thing which had to be explained to me. No charges have been mentioned and I haven't been given the opportunity to request legal advice. Why would that be?"

Now flustered, and getting little in the way of assistance from the man to his right or from the supposed individuals behind the mirror, the Inspector issued an instruction for the duty solicitor to be summoned and left the room along with his colleague. Watkinson looked at his watch – five fifteen; Tom Skerritt would now be well clear of the library and the documents which he had taken away would probably now back in London at the headquarters of MI5. A simple phone call from one of the operatives collecting the material would be enough to ensure that Watkinson could play out the current scenario to maximum effect. His mobile rang at that precise moment.

"Hello, George Watkinson."

"Fostropp."

"Thank you, goodbye."

The inspector returned to the interview room with the duty solicitor in tow, and they resumed their seats with the legal representative at Watkinson's side.

"Mr Watkinson." The sigh in the man's voice told George all that he needed to know about the state of the questioning to come. He had clearly had a briefing to bring the matter to a conclusion as quickly as possible. "We believe that you have removed some documents from the Cheltenham library, and if so are guilty of theft."

"So, you're calling me a thief, is that correct?" He looked to one side at the solicitor who made no comment.

"We can clear this up very quickly if you would allow a search of your person and property."

"You have a warrant for this?" Watkinson was not about to make this easy – he wanted to see who was behind the mirror, and knew that if he frustrated the policeman long enough that person would be forced into revealing him or her self.

"No, but I'm sure that the duty solicitor will tell you that it would be the easiest course of action to take."

Watkinson looked once more at the man at his side, not that he needed the advice since he was well versed in all matters relating to legal proceedings, the solicitor smiled weakly and nodded.

"Very well, let's get on with it. What is it that you think I have stolen?"

"The librarian has reported the disappearance of a package of old documents from the room where you carried out your research."

"I find that difficult to understand" said Watkinson "since I was only out of the building for a matter of moments when your men turned up. There would not have been time to conduct a thorough search of the room."

There followed a tense and silent stand-off when none of the three in the room made any comment. George Watkinson sat with his arms folded in a defiant posture waiting for the inspector to continue with the charade. His gamble paid off; the door opened and a smartly dressed man in a suit entered the room and introduced himself as Alan Mason. The duty solicitor whispered something into George's ear and the search commenced. Satisfied that nothing of any note was concealed on George's person, attention turned to the briefcase. Watkinson placed it in the centre of the table and waved a hand theatrically across it.

"Please help yourselves, but I must insist that any damage be paid for."

Finding nothing incriminating inside the case itself, the inspector began tapping the bottom and the lid. Hearing an echo he looked up at Watkinson who shrugged. A knife was produced and the lining of the case slit to reveal a second compartment. Alan Mason' initial interest soon faded when the space appeared to contain nothing.

"Ok, so nothing here" Watkinson pointed at himself "and nothing here" now pointing at the case. "Mind telling me now what this is really all about?"

Alan Mason shook his head at the inspector and left the room without saying another word. The inspector slammed the case shut and left the room telling George that he was free to go. The duty solicitor was packing away his things when Watkinson stopped him leaving the room.

"Whether they really know who I am or not is inconsequential, but you are governed by a code of ethics and a set of rules. You failed me today, and I will hold you to account for that."

"I don't understand; this was a simple case of mistaken identity. The case will be paid for. Who the hell do you think you are?"

From the inside pocket of his jacket, Watkinson removed a business card and gave it to the man, watching him pale as he read the words.

"Tell your senior partner that I will see him at my offices in Whitehall tomorrow morning at nine sharp, and make sure that you come along with him. It's time that you people realised who runs this country."

Once more out in the open air, Watkinson called the mobile number which Tom Skerritt had given him. He smiled as he returned the phone to his pocket – there would be plenty of time tomorrow to go through the files in detail but first he would take the time to catch up with Roger and Madeline Fretwell.

21

*I*t had been too easy, much too easy. The old man lay dead or dying on the floor, he didn't care which and the package which he had been summoned to collect was now safely in his hands. Alan Mason would be satisfied at last, and he was an extremely difficult man to please sometimes. Tom Skerritt hadn't seen it coming and welcomed the man in the dark suit into the safe house with a smile on his face. It hadn't lasted beyond the sight of the silenced pistol which appeared from nowhere and there was no time to make a run for it. Three shots in quick succession had taken care of any possible resistance and he picked up the mobile into which the old man had already punched a number. Mimicking his voice had been a piece of cake, and with the guy who had accompanied him to the house already taken care of, it only remained for the bodies to be concealed in the property, and he would be on his way.

The mole had been 'sleeping' within MI5 for a number of years and had managed to remain undetected despite Watkinson's meticulous screening techniques. This had been his first real field assignment; all the others had been information gathering jobs and he had been getting very bored of late. Today had reignited his interest and he was off back to London with the package within half an hour after a quick clean down of the kill site.

For an old man, Tom Skerritt was very resilient but three bullets at close range had been too much for him. With his last breath he had tried to reach the discarded mobile phone to alert George Watkinson to the day's events but his effort was all in vain. With the realisation that this was the end, he rolled back on to his side and as the darkness began to gather around him he smiled one last smile at the stupidity of the young man now speeding away from the village. By the time he arrived at his destination and the package had been unwrapped it would be too late to rectify the mistake which he had made.

He must have been told to check the contents of the bundle, and clearly knew what to look for as the grin on his face had revealed. The information contained within was genuine enough and having read some of the files, Skerritt had finally realised the potentially devastating effect that their publication would have. What the assassin had failed to appreciate was the quality of the paper, modern A4 Snow White copy grade paper, and not the slightly yellow tinged and flimsy stuff which was prevalent on both sides of The Channel during the war. An unforced laugh at the rage which would be meted out when the error was realised was enough to bring down the curtain on a life which had been rich in its quality and pattern. Tom Skerritt's head rolled to one side, and he slowly slipped away.

The journey to Bishop's Cleve had been taken via a copy shop on the outskirts of Cheltenham. Here, for a relatively small fee, Tom Skerritt had photocopied every one of the documents in each of the files and replaced the originals with the facsimiles. Once done, those originals were consigned via courier to George Watkinson in Whitehall, and the way bill sent to the same place under separate cover. His instincts had always been to trust no-one until proven otherwise, and they had served him well right to the end.

One call from the now fast departing saloon car had Alan Mason grinning with satisfaction in his office at New Scotland Yard, but a final report to his superior would be delayed until the documents were actually in his hands – there had already been too many slip ups and one more could well cost him his job, or maybe worse. It was then that his personal mobile phone brought a shrill warning sound to his ear.

"Mason!" he snapped. Keen to maintain his outwardly sullen demeanour, this was the way in which all callers to that line were greeted.

"Sir, it's the Farnley woman – she's gone."

"Gone? Gone where, and how? I thought you had that end of things all taken care of. When did this happen?"

"A few days ago sir. We've been trying to find her since she got away, but she seems to have vanished."

"You bloody fools! Can't I trust you to do anything? What about the husband?"

"Dead sir. We eliminated him after she disappeared. No-one will find the body."

"Did you get the debriefing finished? What about all her files – are you sure that we got everything from the house in Cleethorpes?"

"It was almost impossible to get anything verbally from her sir, but we did clear the property of all the Farnleys' stuff. It's all under lock and key now."

"Get back here pronto all of you, and make sure that the place is clean before you leave. I don't want any more loose ends up there, understand?"

"Of course sir."

Mason slammed the mobile down on his desk and muttered a series of well-chosen curses under his breath. Miranda Farnley was one of his most resourceful operatives and had the ability to remain under cover for an indefinite time. She would take some finding now that she was on the loose and free of the ball and chain that was Gregory Farnley; she may even try to go over to the other side. With the information which she had gathered over the years, that could be an extremely embarrassing situation and had to be prevented at all costs. He had to admit that he had not enjoyed closing her down on the east coast, but that idiot husband of hers had screwed up for the last time. She had carried him for a number of years, and Mason had only tolerated Gregory as a result of the high regard in which Miranda was held as an agent by the organisation.

He decided that now was not the best time to provide the Whitehall mandarin with an update on the situation – far better to wait for the delivery of the papers from Cheltenham and be sure that the matter was closed than be caught out again. He was still smarting from the last reprimand which had been meted out to him. He looked at his watch – just after five and the mole would be approaching the M25 within the next fifteen minutes. There was time for a quick meal before returning to his office and the luxury of a detailed examination of the files which, once destroyed, would guarantee the organisation's plans for the future of Britain – a Britain which had died since the sixties, a Britain in which all respect seemed to have vanished and which was now lurching dangerously towards anarchy and intolerance.

He had joined the organisation ten years ago after a number of high profile failures of the judicial system to deal with sections of society seemingly hell bent on its destruction. Its manifesto appealed to his sense of 'correctness' and even its right wing, almost fascist, leanings did not worry him too much. You couldn't make an omelette without breaking a few eggs, and no-one would dare to reinstate the kind of regimes that were common under Hitler and Mussolini. No, there would be checks and balances within the new system to prevent that kind of dictatorship emerging, and after a year or two of pain the public would have democracy returned to them in a form which had not existed for almost forty years.

Alan Mason was far from naïve and realised that, as the saying goes 'Power corrupts and absolute power corrupts absolutely.' Nevertheless he felt that the risk of a 'coup d'etat' was worth taking when the long term benefits were so great. A shrill warbling from his mobile interrupted the train of thought.

"Collins, I have the package and I'm at Euston station. Where shall we meet?"

"Go to the Jarvis Hyde Park and wait for me in the bar. I'll be about fifteen minutes."

Mason knew Collins by sight. He was one of the up and coming, young and thrusting operatives desperate to make his mark in what he too saw as a new order. They adjourned to a quiet corner of the bar and Collins deposited the parcel on a table. Mason smiled as he undid the brown wrapping paper which Tom Skerritt had used to keep the documents safe. That smile vanished in an instant when the parcel was opened.

"What's this?"

"Sorry sir, what do you mean?"

"This" He pointed at the photocopies.

"I don't follow. You said to recover the documents from the old man, and those are what he handed over."

"Damn fool, don't you realise that these aren't the originals? They're on modern paper. The ones we're looking for are over forty years old."

Collins face fell as he realised how stupid he had been. One look inside the package would have been enough to tell him that Skerritt still had the original files hidden somewhere. Now that he was dead, all chance of recovering them seemed to have gone along with any chance of his own progression within the organisation.

22

*L*ife for Julie and Doug Martin had returned to some semblance of normality following the rather frenetic activity of the past few weeks. Despite being warned that their home may have been the subject of some interest to the Farnleys nothing seemed to be out of place and the neighbours had noticed no unusual activity during the period in which they had both been absent. Nevertheless it had taken them a while to become comfortable in their own surroundings once again. Elizabeth and James had quizzed them both unmercifully about the events of the preceding week when they had been carted off to Doug's parents.

Doug, though initially not keen to become involved in his wife's apparent obsession with the matter, had found himself being inexorably drawn into what he saw as some sort of '39 Steps' adventure, and had to admit to himself that he had quite enjoyed the excitement of the chase up and down the country. Enough was enough though, and he had managed to persuade Julie that now was the time to let the whole thing drop and leave those in authority to deal with the matter. She, however, though outwardly in agreement with her husband, still harboured a desire to see the thing right through to the very end and it was with a sense of some disappointment that she now saw herself left behind in the wake of George Watkinson, Tom Skerritt and the Fretwells.

The August Saturday evening was drawing to a close and Doug was busy packing away the barbeque after a number of their friends had returned to their homes. Julie had finished tidying up inside and now sat before the television with a glass of Shiraz and the TV guide. With James in his room and Elizabeth in the bath, she was winding down in her customary fashion when the doorbell rang, and rang again and then a third time before she was even on her feet.

"Alright, alright keep your hair on; I'm coming, where's the fire?" She strode purposefully to the front door, now irritated that her little bit of peace and quiet had been disrupted.

She couldn't see who it was through the frosted glass of the door panel and her first instinct was to put the security chain on before opening it. Doug appeared at that moment, summoned by the same impatient warbling of the bell, and as he was at her side Julie decided it safe to take the risk and turned the catch. A female form pushed the door wide and hurried past both of them as they stood aside in surprise.

"Close that door quickly before someone sees me here!" The command was barked out in such commanding tones that Julie obeyed without hesitation before turning to confront the person who had so dramatically invaded their home.

"Miranda! What the hell……?"

"Shut up and listen; it's important that you understand what's been going on since you left the east coast."

"Just one damn minute, woman" Doug stepped in "Who the hell do you think you are bursting in here like this. I should throw you out on your ear after what you and that husband of yours have been up to."

"Back off! You have no idea what you have got yourselves involved in, and it's as much in your interest as it is mine that you listen to what I have to say."

Doug took a look outside and around the house under the guise of tidying away after their party during the afternoon, and came back inside happy that there was no-one in the immediate vicinity who looked to be threatening. They went into the lounge and Julie drew the curtains at Miranda's request before the Farnley end of the story began to unfold. To be fair to Miranda, she was open and candid with the Martins about the role which she and Gregory had played in the search for Roger and Madeline Fretwell, and freely admitted lying to Julie in the hope of obtaining information as to their whereabouts.

"So you're on the run then?" Julie asked, still suspicious of the woman "How did you manage to find us? We never told you where we live."

"No, but the manager of the caravan site was quite willing to provide that information when put under the correct amount of pressure." There was clearly a 'hard as nails' side to Miranda Farnley which neither of them had ever seen in Cleethorpes. "And I left him with a reminder of what could happen to him if he ever crossed me."

Miranda told them both of the abduction of her and Gregory, the clearing of the house on Queen's Drive and a trip under cover of darkness somewhere to the north, possibly Yorkshire, where they were kept in a remote farmhouse and held for questioning by a team of agents working for 'Control' as she put it. Gregory had cracked quite easily under the pressure, something which she should have foreseen years before, and there being no further use for him he was taken out one evening and never returned. He was almost certainly now dead and hidden where discovery would be extremely unlikely. She herself had held out under a barrage of psychological pressure, and it was during one of the breaks in the interrogation that she had managed to slip away.

The men questioning Miranda had obviously not been briefed too well about her resourcefulness, and whilst alone with one of them one evening when the other two had taken themselves off to a local pub she made her move. Distasteful as it was, she made an obvious play for her guard and once close enough managed to immobilise him with a well aimed kick between the legs. He hadn't even reached the floor in his agony before a chair came crashing down on the back of his head. Gathering up a few essential items she left the property and headed for the main road where she flagged down a passing motorist heading for the nearest town. It had taken her the better part of two days to make the journey to Solihull and the Martins home, and a combination of sleeping rough and begging lifts had got her as far as Birmingham Airport; from there she had walked and the state of her appearance bore testimony to the rigours of the whole trip.

Julie was unsure of her next step and after speaking quietly to Doug, decided to call Tom Skerritt on the mobile number which he had given to her at the start of the journey from Tewkesbury to

Morecambe. The call rang out for what seemed an unusually long time before an unfamiliar voice answered at the other end.

"Yes?"

"Tom? Is that you?"

"Who is this please?"

"Julie Martin. Look, where's Tom Skerritt? I need to speak to him urgently. Are you a friend of his?"

"In a way Mrs Martin. This is George Watkinson. I'm afraid I have some bad news. Tom Skerritt is dead; he was shot a few days ago whilst waiting for one of my agents at a safe house. What is it that you wanted to discuss with him?"

"My God, no! What happened?"

"That's a matter of national security as I am sure you will understand. Has something happened to you and Doug?"

"No, that's not the problem. Miranda Farnley has turned up on our doorstep. She says she escaped from kidnappers and that they've killed her husband. I think she wants to talk to you as soon as possible. She's very frightened and I don't feel like keeping her here for any longer than is necessary."

"Alright. I know where you live. Do not open the door to anyone until I get there. Better still turn off all your lights and stay in a room where no-one can see any of you. I'm leaving my office now and I'll be there in a couple of hours."

Julie and Doug returned to the lounge where Miranda had fallen asleep after her tiring journey. Doug closed the curtains, covered her with a blanket and they sat down to wait for Watkinson after ensuring that the children were safe in their rooms. There was no doubt in Julie's mind that all efforts would be made to find Miranda and that anyone standing in the way would be dealt with as mere collateral damage. With all the lights now extinguished they sat and listened nervously to each and every sound throughout the next two hours.

For George Watkinson this was an enormous break. Not only had he received the original files which Tom Skerritt had wisely posted to him, but he now had within his grasp a significant cog in the organisation's wheel and the value of the information which she held could be inestimable. It almost made up for the loss of Tom and the other two agents outside Cheltenham – almost, but not quite. With a driver and two armed guards he was off the M25 in half an hour and away up the M40 towards Birmingham; one more step forward in his battle against the secret Fascist plot to take control of Britain.

23

*A*lan Mason had no way of knowing where Miranda Farnley had gone, and the agents responsible for her being kept captive had found no trace of an escape route. She had taken great care to cover her tracks by a tactic of doubling back several times before heading off for the nearest road. She had chosen her mode of transport very carefully too, selecting a long distance container lorry on its way south instead of a local vehicle which could have resulted in her being remembered and identified by the county police force. Having hurriedly packed a number of essential items of clothing she was sure that the first part of her journey would not cause too many raised eyebrows, and a quick change in some woods just off the main road made certain that her clean attire should get her through the first part of her escape.

All around him Mason felt that the situation was degenerating into some kind of Keystone Cops slapstick, and the meticulous plans developed over the past few years were starting to fall apart. His boss within the civil service would require some very substantial answers to a series of pointed questions at some time in the very near future, and losing sight of the German files was not a matter which was likely to go down too well. He was certain however, that they were quite safe within the confines of MI5 for the time being and it was not beyond the bounds of possibility that, even at this late stage, they could be recovered by some covert action. The main issue at present was Miranda, the knowledge which she possessed and the damage which she could inflict if it got into the wrong hands. No doubt there would be an attempt to contact the security services and with Skerritt dead, her only real option would be the young couple who had originally set the ball rolling in Cleethorpes.

That the Farnleys had failed to track them as the family car returned home was unfortunate, but enquiries within the organisation's network in the West Midlands had turned up a small number of possible addresses within the Birmingham area. The Martins had let slip that they lived in Solihull and one of those addresses had appeared on the list supplied to him. He was currently on his way there along with a small convoy of vehicles capable of sealing off the immediate area of the family's home. He looked at his watch, he found himself doing a lot of that now, and estimated the time of arrival to be within the next couple of hours. Surely this time nothing could go wrong – after all, who could they possibly call for help?

Of the two sets of vehicles homing in on the Solihull area, George Watkinson was approximately forty-five minutes ahead of his adversary and now on the final approach to Junction 3a of the M40 which would take him the relatively short distance up the M42 to its intersection with the A41. From that point he would be minutes away from the Martin home. He made the call to Julie.

"Mrs Martin, be ready with all of your family in about fifteen minutes. Take one set of clothing with you and wait in your hallway. My team will seal off the road until we have you all safely in the car. Tell no-one what is happening otherwise our entire situation may be compromised. Do not tell Miranda who we are or what you have arranged. If she is sleeping it would be better to leave her alone until we arrive. I'll take it from there, OK?"

Julie put down the phone and assembled her family and two small overnight bags. A short while later three vehicles pulled up just outside in the street. A quiet rap on the front door brought Doug to the letterbox. A voice outside spoke only one word and he wondered at the idiosyncratic nature of the secret service and their choice of passwords.

"Fostropp"

"Mr Harris?"

"No Mr Martin, but it's good that you're on the ball with your checking. It's George Watkinson, and if you don't mind we need to move quickly. If you could let me in I will deal with Mrs Farnley."

George Watkinson managed to appear smart and businesslike at any hour of the day and swept past the Martins and into their lounge where Miranda was just stirring from the only proper sleep she had experienced for a number of days.

"Mrs Farnley good evening, I understand that there are some matters which you wish to discuss with me. My name is George Watkinson and I am the head of MI5."

Miranda, bleary eyed and still in another world, allowed herself to be steered gently out of the Martins' house and into one of the waiting cars. The Martins and their still sleeping children were ushered into another of the vehicles, and with the property now secured and appearing as normal as it could, they headed out of Solihull and back to the motorway. Unbeknown to both Watkinson and the now arriving Alan Mason, the convoys passed each other going in opposite directions just south of Junction 16 of the M40 at Lapworth. Watkinson had already decided that the best place for Miranda Farnley would be within the bowels of MI5 itself and the vehicles all made their way back to London until he could be certain that the Martins' home would be safe enough for them to return. Having left instructions for a watch to be kept upon the property by Special Branch, he would know almost immediately of any outside interest in the family.

Alan Mason, on the other hand, was left cursing once more the short comings of his organisation in the field. Arriving in Solihull not long after Watkinson's convoy had departed; he fumed at the discovery that he had missed them by so short a margin. Careful not to arouse too much suspicion with neighbours, quiet enquiries were made as to the whereabouts of the Martin family but no-one remembered hearing any departing vehicles, and he was left with the only course of action being that of a return to base. Not for the first time though, his contacts within the police force were to throw him a lifeline.

Watkinson's fast moving convoy heading south east down the M40 had attracted the attention of the Buckinghamshire police near the town of Denham, and Mason's sources had informed him that although they could hold the party for around half an hour on speeding charges, it would be impossible to delay them for any longer without creating a significant incident. There was no doubt as to the identity of the passengers, as Watkinson's description had been circulated to all organisation contacts within the force since the trip across the Pennines from Morecambe. This, Mason decided, could be his last chance to intercept Miranda Farnley before she disappeared from his reach for good. With immunity from police involvement the driver of the chasing car put his foot down, pulled into the overtaking lane and gunned the engine to 120mph as the tide of traffic before it parted like the Red Sea. Mason pulled out his mobile phone and issued instructions to his normal contact.

"Collins, where are you? I've got an urgent job."

"Home as usual; I'm off duty today. What is it, where and when?"

He gave the assassin descriptions of the vehicles, their registration plates and the occupants of the target car. The location of the hit would be down to circumstances and opportunity at the time, but Mason impressed upon the man the importance of not allowing Miranda to reach the capital.

"Remember, it's just her I want taking care of. No need to go gun happy like last time, alright?"

"Got it boss."

George Watkinson's party, at this time, was stationary on the hard shoulder just north of junction 1 – another mile or so and they would have been off the motorway and out of the reach of its eagle-eyed squad cars. With three sets of documents to check the police were taking their time, and although all three drivers admitted to the offences listed to them progress was excruciatingly slow. Watkinson had to resist the temptation to exert his authority and get the vehicles moving once again – that would have drawn attention to all of them, and the last thing he needed at present was the whereabouts of his escapee to become known. After what seemed an age, and with the necessary tickets issued, they were once more on their way, and left the M40 at the Denham intersection.

Collins was out of his house in Bayswater and on his Kawasaki in full gear within fifteen minutes and heading for the A40. Allowing for the forced delay on the convoy which Mason had organised, he planned to lay in wait for Watkinson's car on Westway in Shepherds Bush – an area which would provide him with any number of possible escape routes. He had been sitting astride the motorbike for around twenty minutes when the first car appeared at the junction with Old Oak Road some fifty yards from his position. Letting all three vehicles pass him by, he slipped into the line of traffic and made his way carefully up to the bumper of the trailing car. The traffic lights on the main road should provide him with the opportunity he was after, and one or two of them were notoriously slow at changing.

They had passed through three junctions when traffic ground to a halt at one particular set of lights which had failed completely. A uniformed officer was directing the flow and it wasn't long before a man answering Watkinson's description exited the middle vehicle and made his way to the front of the queue, presumably to impress upon the constable in charge the importance of his journey. Edging up the outside of the line of traffic, the motor cyclist pulled up level with the still open door of the car and removed a silenced pistol from the inside of his leathers. Looking around briefly for any witnesses he released the safety catch, leaned forward for one glance inside the rear seats to ensure that his target was the correct one, and fired three shots at point blank range. Watkinson stopped dead in his tracks fifty yards away and turned around. He had heard the tell-tale 'pop-pop-pop' of the gun and caught a brief glimpse of the Kawasaki turning right across the line of oncoming vehicles and down Sundew Avenue. With no chance of catching the rider he raced back to the car and looked inside the rear seats. Miranda Farnley was dead; she had taken three hits, two to the torso and one to the head any of which could have proven fatal. There was blood all over the back of the car and without hesitation Watkinson was inside, and the three vehicles were out of the line of traffic and turning right along Sundew Avenue via the same route as that taken by the gunman.

They arrived at HQ twenty minutes later and arrangements were made for accommodation for Julie, Doug and their children. Miranda Farnley's body was taken to the local mortuary under a thick cloak of secrecy and arrangements made for a covert funeral and disposal; ballistics would later match the bullets to the gun used on Madeline Fretwell. Watkinson cursed his luck at the loss of an invaluable source of information and despite all stops being pulled out no trace could be found of the motor cyclist. He now had only the files from Roger Fretwell and even they could no longer be considered as safe. He needed a back up plan and one in the form of a high class forger immediately sprang to mind.

24

*S*olomon Wiseman had taken over his father's printing company when the old man died in 1972. They had come to Britain in the 1930's, fleeing from Nazi persecution in Germany and had set up home in London's East End. The print works had somehow survived the Blitz and boomed in the post war era, becoming one of the capital's top quality printing concerns. Business had taken a nose dive however with the movement of the Fleet Street trade to Wapping in the 1980s, and Solly had to find another outlet for his talents to subsidise his regular customers. He did. A lifetime in the trade had taught him the secrets of producing high class 'official' documents and for a price, nothing was out of reach.

Watkinson had crossed paths with Wiseman at a number of official functions – he was, after all, an upstanding pillar of the local neighbourhood. Solly had always taken great care never to step over what had come to be regarded as an undrawn line in the sand. He had fought shy of any involvement with the IRA or the UVF during The Troubles, and the security services had always kept a wary eye on his activities. Though George despised any kind of shady trade, he was constantly aware that it was not always in the best interests of law enforcement to drive the likes of Solomon Wiseman out of the capital. He had been a useful source in the past, and was about to become one once more; taking care to avoid normal working hours he was waiting as the man's car pulled slowly out of the factory gates. Watkinson flagged him down and got in.

"Mr Watkinson! Such a pleasure to see you again after all this time. Tell me now, what can a man such as I do for Her Majesty's security forces this time?"

George forced back a smile as he listened to the man's opening speech, one which never changed and which was always the preamble to more serious discussions once the niceties were dispensed with.

"Alright Solly, cut it out. We have serious business to conduct. Let's go to your place and I'll tell you what I need."

Once inside the imposing detached house in St Johns Wood Road, Watkinson laid out before Wiseman the files which Roger Fretwell had brought back from Germany in 1945. The Jew's faced changed the moment he caught sight of the swastika on the first page; his frown deepened when he recognised the Gestapo lettering which surrounded it. Standing up abruptly he poured a double measure of malt for them both and returned to the table.

"Where did you get these?" The voice had changed dramatically from that of the genial businessman who had left the factory gates a short time earlier.

"That's not important. What matters is that they remain in the right hands, and at the moment that cannot be guaranteed. I need copies, and they have to be good enough to pass the most detailed examination."

"And what will you do with these 'copies' may I ask? After all, there are other parties who will certainly be interested in their acquisition for the same purposes as I suspect you intend them."

"No need for you to concern yourself about that Solly my friend, just concentrate on the job at hand. The quality of the work will need to stand up to the closest scrutiny; I assume that you are still able to match that standard?"

"I'm a forger Mr Watkinson, the best there is. If I can't do this job no-one can, But I'd like to know a little bit more about the papers than you have already told me."

George Watkinson was going to have to trust the man, and to be fair to Wiseman he had never let the side down before. Keeping as much back as possible, and without revealing the names of those involved in the discovery, he sat the printer down and recounted the events of the past few months. Throughout the story Solly sat stone faced and silent apart from a few brief interjections for clarification. His father's family had suffered badly at the hands of the Nazis, and as far as he was aware his side of it was the only one to have escaped the Holocaust; they had lost many family members and friends at Auschwitz. Having long craved some form of revenge on those responsible he now had that power within his grasp only to find it denied to him.

"So what are you going to do with the copies?"

"They, my friend, will be the bait I am going to set in the trap to catch those responsible for the deaths of at least three people in my team, and also for the persecution that went on during the war."

"I'm sure that I can achieve the second objective with far more efficiency, if you'd give me the chance."

"No. I don't want Mossad involved in any of this. I remember all the fuss over Eichmann in South America and the raid on Entebbe airport in July 1976. If your guys get a hold of this paperwork they'll be in with their hob nailed boots. I want the entire organisation taken down not driven underground. We won't move against anyone until we are sure that nothing will be missed."

"Alright Mr Watkinson, have it your way. Such a pity though."

"Sure you can get hold of the right materials?"

"Oh yes. The paper will be easy, there are still available supplies of pre-war quality and I can age it down to the exact year you need. The inks were pretty crude in those days and I can make some up to match the colour and body of the print. Making up the swastika and the headings will be OK, I'll do the compositing myself and the photographs can be replicated using a computer program that's just come on to the market. Don't worry I won't let you down."

"In that case, I'm sure you won't mind me coming along with you. Those are the originals and after what they've cost other people I'm not letting them out of my sight for a moment."

"Mr Watkinson, and I thought that you trusted me!" Solly smiled and led the way down to the basement workshop where he did his 'private' work for a few select customers.

True to his word, George Watkinson remained at the Wiseman home for the next two days whilst Solly laboured away at the task. The man's skill had never been in doubt, but George was impressed by the attention to detail and meticulous, almost painstaking way in which the first proofs were prepared. Solly himself destroyed a number of attempts before presenting the first draft to the head of MI5. He pondered over the few pages which Wiseman had manufactured, constantly comparing them in detail to the originals. When the final copies were before him, he had to admit that, if he hadn't actually kept hold of the originals himself it would have been nigh on impossible to tell them apart from the forgeries.

"Solly, you've surpassed yourself this time. There's no way anyone would suspect these weren't the real thing."

"Just another job, Mr Watkinson. Now, about my fee."

"Normal rates Solly old son, normal rates." Then he thought again "Plus a twenty-five per cent bonus if the plan comes off."

"Very kind I'm sure" He smiled "Well if that's all, I'll be getting on with the rest of the job. You can put the kettle on if you've nothing else to do."

George sat back to wait whilst the printer carried out the contract, and the seeds of a plan to rein in the whole organisation began to germinate. That there was a mole within MI5 he was certain, and the placing of the copies could have the benefit of flushing out whoever was passing information to outside sources. The entire team were aware of the importance of the files, and he wouldn't have to be too careless about where he stored them before someone took it upon themselves to effect a recovery. Steve Marshall, his second in command, was the only one he really trusted with this information and the two of them could set up the department for a break in quite easily.

He wasn't sure how long he had been daydreaming when Wiseman heaved a huge sigh and stepped back from the Heidelberg press he had been working on.

"That's it. All printed and dried, cut to the correct size and aged so my grandmother would think they were her own. I think you'll be pleased with them."

"And the originals?"

"Oh yes, mustn't forget them must we? Be such a pity if they ended up in the wrong hands wouldn't it?"

Solly smiled. He knew Watkinson hadn't taken his eyes off them for a minute. Sliding them into the deep inside pocket of his overcoat, George bade a farewell and left the premises.

25

*T*he descent on to the roof from the helicopter had been easy enough, and he smiled at the mole's concerns for his accuracy. He told the man he could land on a paving slab given calm weather and tonight had been perfect. Carefully folding away the parachute canopy, he approached the access door to the stairway which would take him to the offices below. He knew it would most likely be locked, but gave it a gentle tug anyway. The lock held firm and he took out a set of tools from the small bag he had brought along. Inserting a narrow metal fillet into the small gap between door and jamb, he released the locking mechanism on the other side and eased it open, listening for the slightest hint of any sound from within. Satisfied that no-one was about, he donned a pair of night vision goggles and descended the pitch black stairway to the first level.

The mole had provided a detailed schematic of the top floor where the target office lay, and it took no time at all to locate the correct corridor. At every turn he stopped and listened, and although confident that his black one piece suit would conceal him in the shadows, there would be no point in taking unnecessary risks now that he was inside the building. Silently he padded along until he stood before the door indicated on the plan. There was no name or number to indicate the occupant of the room, but his instructions were that this was the office of George Watkinson, head of MI5. The task was simple; break in, remove a package locked in the second drawer down on the right hand side of the desk and get out in as short a time as possible.

The office door itself presented no great difficulty and he was soon at the desk facing the window. With moonlight streaming in through the half closed blinds, there was no further need for the goggles and he removed them. For the first time his face was fully revealed and although he was completely unaware, a series of remote cameras were now recording his every move, and from a variety of angles. The drawer did not respond to any of his specialised tools and remained stubbornly shut. He sat back in the chair and listened once more. There was complete silence and the sound of his heart pounding away was the only thing he could hear. Burglary was one thing, but breaking into the headquarters of the security services was apt to make the pulse race. With no other option, and now certain that any noise would go undetected, he resorted to the crudest of the burglary trade's implements. Taking the crowbar from his bag, he inserted it under the desk lip and pushed downwards with all his weight. A loud 'crack' erupted like gunfire and he froze momentarily, poised for flight.

He stood perfectly still for what seemed like an age before opening the now wrecked drawer. There on top of a set of books was the envelope which he had been told to remove. It was brown and bore the crest of Her Majesty's Security Services, but the wording 'Top Secret' was the giveaway. One brief look inside the package was enough to tell him that he had the correct merchandise, and it disappeared into the depths of his bag. Ensuring that all surfaces had been wiped clean he made his way out of the office, carefully wiping the door handle on his way past. Retracing his steps in the same careful manner as he had used only a brief time before, he was soon back up on the roof. Packing the parachute into its casing, and leaving no clues as to his presence on the roof he was over the edge and climbing down the outside of the building towards the darkness and anonymity of the London streets. Ten minutes later he was gone.

George Watkinson and Steve Marshall emerged from the office at the end of the corridor where the break in had occurred. Marshall had spent the better part of the past two days setting up a set of surveillance cameras in Watkinson's office. They had waited patiently each night since the papers had been 'carelessly' left in the desk drawer, and were sure that the mole would be aware of the security risk surrounding the act. Tonight their patience had paid off and with a collective holding of breath now lubricated by several measures of the scotch which emerged from the bottom right hand drawer, they toasted the success of the operation.

The burglar would not go undetected; neither would he be intercepted immediately as a number of cars had been strategically positioned at all points of exit from the building. A burst of static from Watkinson's belt radio now broke the conversation.

"Aplha One – target acquired. Over"

"Roger Aplha One. Maintain visual only and proceed as instructed. All units – close in with Alpha One and go to second locations. Out"

Watkinson hooked the radio back on to his belt and sat down. Whether the burglar would make contact with his principal tonight was uncertain, but whatever course of action he took would be watched carefully from a number of vantage points, and the worst case scenario would be the discovery of his base.

"Any idea who the mole is, Sir?"

"Not yet, Steve. There's been a leak for a while now, but this is the first time I've had the chance to draw him or her out into the open. We'll see what happens when we do pick this guy up but that won't be until we know where the files are going. Better get this desk fixed though before my scotch goes walkabout."

The burglar had made his getaway on a motorcycle and the four tailing unmarked cars took it in turns to follow him across the capital. The man was clever and doubled back upon himself a number of times before being confident of heading home. That journey took forty-five minutes and he eventually turned into a property in the Maida Vale area of the city. With the vehicles posted at either end of the street the lead car radioed the position back to Watkinson.

"Ok, stay with him and take it in turns to sleep. As soon as he leaves the place or anyone else goes in, I want to know and we'll take it from there."

There was no activity at the address for the rest of the night, and when morning came the only visitors were the paper boy and the early morning delivery of milk. Strangely, the milkman went inside and communication with all other surveillance teams had everyone on high alert. Half an hour later, agents covering the rear of the premises reported two men leaving via the back door and crossing a number of rear gardens of adjoining properties. They emerged fifty yards further down the street and got into a dark blue Mondeo which pulled away and headed off towards the Edgware Road and central London. Once more the trailing vehicles rotated their position within the traffic to avoid any possibility of detection by the two travellers, and followed the car to Hyde Park where the occupants parked it before crossing towards The Serpentine.

With all six MI5 agents now stationed at various points within the confines of the park, Watkinson headed in that direction along with Steve Marshall. The open space was an ideal place for the burglar to meet those who commissioned the robbery without being overheard, and it was now clear that the sole purpose of the 'milkman' had been to ensure that he was taken to a pre-arranged spot at a given time. The place chosen for the rendezvous however seemed to have been Speakers' Corner and with a large number of the public in attendance it was easy for the agents to close in on the party without becoming conspicuous. The burglar and his driver stood to one side of the range of podiums and constantly scanned the passing crowds for some sign of the person they had arranged to meet.

George Watkinson and Steve Marshall were now in place at the edge of Hyde Park with a clear view of the area, and with the aid of binoculars were able to watch the unfolding events without being seen. Mason himself was keenly aware of the possibility of being intercepted and, without revealing himself to the two waiting for him, had passed them by on three occasions before he was satisfied that the situation was safe. Watkinson's men had picked up his tactic on the second pass and were now focussed in on his movements. The meeting was brief, lasting only a few moments, and a brown package was exchanged for an envelope presumably containing an amount of money. The three then went their separate ways out of the area, and a team followed each one.

Watkinson and Marshall followed Alan Mason who now had the files, and a radio instruction was issued to pick the other two up as soon as they were clear of the park; they would be taken back to MI5 headquarters for questioning. Mason moved with some urgency to a car parked on the northern edge of Hyde Park where a driver sat waiting, but Watkinson managed to note the registration number of the vehicle and issued instructions for the remaining team to follow on and report its progress as they made their way back to his own car.

Alan Mason was feeling cautiously pleased at the capture of what he believed to be the genuine documents, and after a series of manoeuvres designed to shake off any tail, he ordered the driver back to New Scotland Yard, where he picked up a fresh car to take him to the Cabinet Offices in Whitehall. Once there he asked to be shown to the office of the Prime Minister's private secretary and, clearly expected, was escorted there immediately. Watkinson and Marshall had managed to avoid detection and were in position at the end of the street when Mason entered the building.

"What now sir?" Marshall asked. He knew that they couldn't simply barge in and arrest the man, but Watkinson had other ideas. First they needed to know how high the matter went within government.

"Steve, you're going in there to find out who he has gone to see. Find out who he is and where he's gone, but don't follow. Make some excuse and come back out."

Marshall collected an envelope from the car and headed for the Cabinet Office. Once inside he approached the reception desk where he was greeted by a smiling clerk.

"Good morning sir, can I help you?" she asked.

"Yes, er I have some urgent papers for the man who just came in."

"Mr Mason?"

"Yes that's it, but I have to deliver them to him personally. Can you tell me where he is?"

"Well yes, but I'm afraid that you can't go any further, he's with the Prime Minister's private secretary and they've issued instructions not to be disturbed."

"Oh, that's awkward."

"Perhaps if you tell me what it's about I can get a message to him and you can wait for a reply."

"No." Marshall's answer was sharp and blunt, and he noticed the receptionist becoming more than a little concerned. And he had to think quickly. "Look, he smiled sheepishly "I'm from the BBC and it's important that you keep this quiet. We're preparing a 'This Is Your Life' programme on Mr Mason."

"Alan Mason?"

"Yes" Marshall now had his full name "So please don't let anyone know that I've been here asking for him. I can't give you a business card because we're not allowed to, but if you call me on this mobile

121

number when he's about to leave I can make sure that I'm around to catch him."

The woman winked in a conspiratorial manner and smiled knowingly. Marshall's skills at thinking on his feet had paid off once more, and reporting back to Watkinson with the man's name got him a pat on the back for his ingenuity.

"Well done, Steve. Knew you'd come up trumps. Now we can find out exactly who this man is and what he's up to. We might even be able to track him right to the top now. Private Secretary to the PM? Mmmm..."

26

With any danger to Julie and Doug Martin now seemingly gone, George Watkinson had organised their return to Solihull following the assassination of Miranda Farnley and the apparently successful burglary at the headquarters of MI5. Following on from the break-in, those now in possession of what they believed to be the original Nazi files would be less inclined to concern themselves with any third parties who had come into contact with them. MI5 had kept a watchful eye on the Martin home in Solihull for a while, but that activity had now been wound down and Watkinson's attention had been refocused on the recipient of the information, and the means by which it was obtained.

Graham Poundall was a 'facilitator'. He hated the term 'burglar; it seemed so coarse for the type of service which he offered to a select clientele. He would obtain, for an appropriately substantial fee, almost anything which was required by his clients. It could range from money and other easily convertible commodities to works of art. The job just completed was an extension of his curriculum vitae to an area which he had not previously serviced, and his expertise in other areas would, he hoped, conceal him from the list of 'usual suspects' for anyone investigating the removal of the files. His fee had been a cool £50,000 and he had returned later on in the evening from a celebratory night out on the town. When the visitors arrived he had been safe within the arms of Morpheus for a couple of hours.

He surfaced drowsily at the sound of a number of voices coming from somewhere within his bedroom, and was startled to see three figures surrounding him. Considering the amount of alcohol which he had consumed the previous evening he did not put up much of a struggle, and even if sober would not have been able to resist being forcibly removed from his bed. They took him down the stairs and out of the house to an awaiting vehicle which was ticking over at the bottom of his front yard. It was still dark, and knowing that he had come home at around two, he estimated the time to be four or after. They had secured his hands with nylon garden ties, and he was shoved into the back of the car and covered with a blanket. In the darkness of his surroundings, Poundall was not able to reliably estimate the length of the journey or where he was being taken, but some time later they all left the vehicle and with a bag of some kind now over his head he was led into a building which echoed only to the sound of their footsteps.

The room was small, with a table and chairs to one side. There was a bed along the far wall, and a cubicle in the opposite corner which presumably housed the toilet facilities. There were no windows, and it was lit with a single sixty watt bulb; the entire atmosphere was oppressive. They provided him with a set of nondescript clothes and some footwear; up to this point no-one had spoken to him – he could have been in a foreign country as far as he was aware, and remembered a similar scenario in an old black and white film called 'The Ipcress Files'. He was becoming aware of an increasingly strong feeling of unease and the knot now forming in the pit of his stomach told him that he was in trouble. There was no clock in the room, and the passage of time was, he thought, some kind of tool which his captors were intending to use against him.

Apart from regular meals and the provision of fresh toiletries he had no contact with anyone, and the individuals bringing his supplies had clearly been told to avoid any attempt at conversation. He had listened closely at the door on a number of occasions, hoping to glean some information as to his whereabouts or the nature and identity of his abductors, but there had been nothing apart from silence broken by the regular sound of footsteps at meal times. When George Watkinson eventually did come into the room, Graham Poundall was almost at his wits end. He sat down at the table and gestured for Poundall to join him. Opening a brown manila folder he turned several of the pages over, scrutinising each one carefully and making a series of notes in the margins of one or two of them. Closing the folder he looked up at Poundall and removed his spectacles, placing them precisely in front of him.

"Mr Graham Poundall." It was a statement rather than a question, but the burglar was nonetheless very pleased to be addressed after all the time he had been in the room. "I believe that you removed some information from a building in central London recently, information to which neither you nor its recipients were entitled."

"Depends on who wants to know." Poundall had recovered a portion of his damaged confidence and reacted in a confrontational manner quite unsuited to his situation.

"Let's be clear about something Mr Poundall." Watkinson leaned forwards across the table and subjected the man to one of his legendary ice cold stares. His blue/grey eyes seemed to bore into the very being of his captive, and Poundall could feel the back of his throat becoming very dry. He continued.

"You are here at my orders, and as far as the general public are concerned you have simply vanished. No questions will be raised about your disappearance as neighbours have been informed that you have taken a trip abroad – we've even left a note for your milkman!"

Poundall was beginning to shake and was having great difficulty concealing his fear. Watkinson picked up on the change in his body language and forced home the advantage.

"We have CCTV evidence of your activities in stealing a set of files from the premises of the security services, and you could be charged with treason. I confess that I am unsure of the maximum penalty for such a crime but doubt that you will celebrate your seventieth birthday outside the confines of one of Her Majesty's maximum security establishments."

"What do you want? How do I get out of this?"

"Firstly the name of the man or woman who supplied you with the information which enabled you to gain entry into the building, and secondly the location of the documents concerned. Nothing less than that will help your case."

"And if I do, I can go?"

"If you don't the only thing for you to look forward to is the less than convivial surrounding of one of our gaols."

"They'll kill me if I tell you who they are."

"So you do know the identity of your principals."

"Only the man who asked me to do the job in the first place."

"The name of that person is very important to me Mr Poundall, and I am sure that once I have it I can exert a significant amount of influence in your favour."

"I don't know Mr....................?"

"My name is not important, but rest assured that I have your entire future in my hands. With one instruction I can ensure that you never return to your home, and that all trace of your existence there is removed. If you doubt that for one moment you are quite welcome to try my patience – I have all the time in the world."

Poundall sat in silence and Watkinson reopened the folder and made another series of notes. At the end of this he replaced the pen into his top pocket, put his spectacles back into their case, closed the folder and stood up. He knocked once on the door and was halfway through it before the burglar reacted.

"Just a minute, I'll tell you what happened."

"Yes you will Mr Poundall, but not today. I am a busy man and you have had your chance for the moment. Make yourself comfortable and I will come to see you again in another day or so."

It would have been very unusual for a first interrogation to be successful and George Watkinson was not displeased at the way in which the meeting had played out. Poundall was quite definitely on the back foot, disorientated and totally unaware of the serious nature of his situation. A few days spent in his own company would make him a more pliable opponent at their next session. The mole, whoever it was, would almost certainly be aware of the abduction of the burglar, and both George and Steve Marshall were highly skilled in the reading of human reactions. Patience and a sharp eye was all that would be needed in observing the staff within MI5. There would come a time when some small insignificant comment or action would betray the infiltrator in their midst.

Poundall sat back down in his chair and stared at the wall before him. He had severely overplayed his hand and now cursed his own stupidity. These men were clearly secret service and, as such, answerable to none of the forces of law and order with whom he normally came into contact. They could keep him here for as long as they chose and no-one on the outside would be any the wiser. A sudden thought made him shiver. If there was an informant inside their organisation what was there to prevent there being another individual, possibly a hit man, commissioned to silencing him before he had the chance to tell what he knew?

27

Alan Mason's reaction to the news of someone enquiring after him at the Cabinet offices had been one of initial surprise followed by an increasing feeling that something was not right. The receptionist had been unable to conceal the ruse that Steve Marshall had spun about a future screening of 'This is Your Life', and although Mason had initially responded to her coyness with a grand show of humility and self-deprecation, the P.A. to the Prime Minister's private secretary had been more circumspect in the conclusions which she drew from the performance. She was a long-serving Whitehall official and had observed more of the failings of human nature than most gave her credit for. Everything that she saw within the confines of the department found its way inevitably back to her mandarin boss – she was not one to be trifled with and Mason should have known better than to perform as he had done in her presence.

Within an hour of his leaving the Whitehall office, Alan Mason's file had been transferred from central records to the office of the private secretary and was now undergoing the most rigorous scrutiny by a team of the most senior civil servants and business leaders in the country. The faces of the six present were anonymous outside the confines of the department, and their voices were flat in the deliverance of their enquiries.

"Is he to be trusted?"

"He's been with us for over ten years now." The private secretary was the respondent to all questions posed.

"That's not what I asked. Is he to be trusted?"

"His clearance within the organisation is second only to our own and the screening, as for all of us, was meticulous and detailed. I can say no more than that at present."

"Does he pose a risk?" Another face and the entire table turned in his direction. "Is it time to consider a replacement?"

"He has acquired the files for us in very difficult and trying circumstances. The risks he has taken personally have been considerable when you take into account his position within the Met. I believe any action in that direction would be both precipitate and ill-advised at this stage."

"What is there to prevent him from going over to the other side?" The eyes of the table turned once more.

"His loyalty to the aims and objectives of the organisation are beyond question, and where he leads others will certainly follow. He truly believes in our manifesto whilst being unaware of the real depth of its intentions. Were we to take him out now there would be a considerable danger of our losing the potential support which his voice would bring to us. He is one of a number of individuals around the country who can be relied upon to carry through our plans based simply upon their own moral values."

"And would you stake your life on him?" The final question came after a pause of several minutes which had been taken up by a shuffling of papers and a packing of brief cases. The man now standing staring out of the window on to Whitehall was one of a small number of wealthy industrialists who had made their way into the inner circles of government by a variety of methods. There was another pause as all activity in the office ceased and eyes homed in upon the private secretary.

"I have not survived thirty years of transient government by taking unwarranted risks. Mason has reported to me and me alone for the entire length of his career whilst in our service, and not once have I had cause to doubt his word or integrity. Yes, I would trust him with my life; I have done so on a number of occasions already and see no reason to change that now."

There followed a communal murmur and the nodding of several greying heads, but the man at the window simply remained unmoved and silent. All eyes were now upon him and the atmosphere in the room became expectant. He picked up his coat and case, made his way to the door and closed it behind himself. A few moments later the private secretary was alone once again and summoned his personal assistant.

"Yes sir?"

"Marjorie, get me George Watkinson's telephone number please."

"I can call him for you if you wish."

"No, it's late. You get on home, I'll do it myself before I leave. There's nothing desperately urgent about it."

"As you wish sir."

Watkinson had, for a number of years, played a dangerous and difficult game within the corridors of power in Whitehall. His position as head of MI5 gave him access to and influence over the opinions of a number of highly placed civil servants within the mechanism of the government. Though the peoples' representatives were charged with running the country every four to five years, it was through the ranks of an army of civil servants that government effectively took place. The private secretary was at the pinnacle of a small group of such people who constantly relied upon the services of the security forces for their own survival. Watkinson took the call in his own private office and for once, albeit temporarily and without revealing his surprise, was caught completely off guard.

"George, I need to see you immediately on a matter of some urgency. Where can we meet?"

"Well somewhere out of town would be preferable. There's a place outside of Pinner which might fit the bill."

The public house chosen for the rendezvous had nothing which could make it stand out from the crowd, and the two businessmen meeting up for an evening meal drew no more than a cursory glance from the management and the other customers on the premises. The position of their table in the corner gave them both privacy and a good view of the remainder of the restaurant; there would be no chance of being overheard. After serving wine and a starter the waiter retired, giving Watkinson the chance to get down to business.

"All a bit sudden and dramatic Marcus, where's the fire?"

"No fire, at least not yet. What do you know of a man by the name of Alan Mason?"

As leading questions went this was a big one, and Watkinson had to be very careful with his choice of words in reply. It was more than possible that Marcus was the man at the top of the organisation which had recently acquired the copies of the Nazi documents. As yet there was no proof that Mason had even taken the files to Whitehall with him and any decision regarding action at this point would be premature and inadvisable. He had to assume at this juncture that Marcus was simply what he appeared to be – a senior civil servant and nothing more.

"Senior officer within the Metropolitan Police at New Scotland Yard. Off the top of my head and without the files in front of me, I'd say that with him what you see is what you get. I believe he has received a couple of commendations during his career, and by all accounts runs a pretty tight ship. He came up through the ranks in the usual manner and there's nothing to differentiate him from a number of other officers following the same career path. Wasn't he responsible for cracking open that serial killing case last year?" This was a deliberate attempt to side step a potentially awkward line of questioning, and was one of Watkinson's usual ploys when he was unsure of the ground on which he stood.

"Yes, the whole thing looked like getting away from the Met at one stage until he broke the key suspect with an eye witness who came forward at the last moment. So there's nothing with MI5's files to indicate any unusual behaviour patterns?"

"Not as far as I'm aware but I'll check them privately tomorrow and get back to you one way or the other. If he's a rogue we would have spotted it by now and either eliminated him or put him to good use for our own benefit."

The remainder of the evening passed in a more convivial manner and conversation reduced to the level of chit chat. By eleven o'clock both were on their way home, but for George Watkinson there were now considerably more questions than answers about the entire matter of the files which Fretwell had brought home with him at the end of the war. He had been putting off a visit to Roger and Madeline for too long; perhaps now was the time to take a break on the North West coast – he had heard that Morecambe was particularly pleasant at this time of year.

The next day, having read through the MI5 files on both Alan Mason and the private secretary, he was speeding North West on the

Intercity 125 for Manchester and the coast. He needed some time out of the capital to try to rationalise all the actions of the various parties involved in what had become a complicated set of circumstances.

28

With the summer now well behind the seaside resort of Morecambe, Roger and Madeline Fretwell's lives returned, along with those of the rest of the permanent population, to the more sedate level of the off season. They ventured more into the town centre than would have been the case if the place were full of holidaymakers, and mixed readily with the small circle of friends which they had acquired since their move from the South West. The two of them had always enjoyed the holidays spent there when the children were growing up, but had never considered it as a place where they would take up more permanent residence. Madeline in particular longed for the tranquillity of their cottage by the River Avon in Tewkesbury and missed the company of the locals and their idiosyncratic ways. She had not settled in Morecambe and lived for the day when they would be able to return to Gloucestershire. She and Roger had talked many times long into the night about the subject, but until it was deemed safe to go back their concealment in the North West would continue.

With this in mind the unexpected arrival of George Watkinson raised their hopes considerably, and although it was only to be a flying visit he did bring with him the news that they had waited so long to hear. Their cottage had originally been 'sold' to a young couple who were, in fact, members of Watkinson's staff in the region. They would be vacating it very soon for another assignment and with attention now focused elsewhere, he considered it safe for the couple to make their reappearance. Madeline's initial excitement was dampened however by George's insistence that they remain where they were until the end of the year, and to consider the possibility of relocating to her former home in Cleethorpes which had become vacant. When she pressed him for a reason all he would say was that matters had now come to a head, and that action against those responsible for the attack on her was imminent.

The couple were encouraged to make discreet preparations for a move, and to acquaint senior family members of the true facts of the matter. It was, he said, vital that news of her existence was kept under wraps and that contact be restricted to sons and daughters only. Madeline would have agreed to anything on hearing this and threw herself into his arms in grateful thanks. Roger Fretwell's interest, although centred upon the return home had also remained sharply focussed upon the issue of the files, and he plied Watkinson for information on their whereabouts. George had not planned a lengthy stay at their temporary home, but when they both sat down he found that he had no alternative but to follow suit.

Choosing his words carefully, he brought the two of them up to date on events which had taken place since Madeline's brush with what Watkinson was now certain were the agents of Alan Mason. They were shocked at the death of Tom Skerritt and intrigued by the cat and mouse game played out around the 'successful' burglary at MI5. He cautioned them on the subject of confidentiality and gently reminded both that they were strictly prohibited, by their signing of the Official Secrets Act, from discussing anything pertaining to the files with anyone else. It was early evening before he finally managed to excuse himself from the Fretwell's hospitality and after ten by the time he was back at his office and making plans for the next phase of the search for the mole within his department.

29

*D*espite being held in relative comfort, Graham Poundall was not in good spirits when Watkinson resumed his interrogation two days after their initial meeting. He was edgy and had developed a nervous twitch, probably due to the lengthy spells in solitary confinement without human contact. His eyes darted around the room and he shifted his position at the table a number of times before Watkinson placed a tape recorder on the table, switched it on and finally addressed him.

"Well Mr Poundall, have you had enough time to consider your situation? I mean, we can give you a further interval if you choose."

"No! No, thank you." The words were snapped out as if Poundall expected his captor to leave the room again at the slightest provocation.

"Very good. Before we go any further let me make things perfectly clear to you. The documents which you removed from my office were of absolutely no use to anyone, although I am sure that your contact led you to believe otherwise."

Poundall's face fell and he sat for a while with his head in his hands. When he looked up again at Watkinson his face had paled considerably. If he got caught, they had said, all he would have to do was deny any knowledge of the break in and the police would be forced to release him without charge within a very short space of time. The man before him however was not a policeman.

"What do you want from me? I mean, I thought the police were suppose to charge you if they pulled you in for anything."

"Mr Poundall" Watkinson smiled disarmingly "I am not a policeman nor are you under arrest, but be assured that until I find out what I need to know, you will remain my guest. You were set up. The person who planned the break in is working covertly within my organisation and it is very important that I find out his or her identity."

Graham Poundall knew that he had few options remaining. He had been left in no doubt by his principal that, once agreed, failure in the task would not be tolerated; neither would they allow disclosure of any material facts to go unpunished; either way he was a dead man. His contact had mentioned another name at MI5 and he decided to offer this up as a means of extricating himself from the situation; he had to make it look good though.

"I have a wife and children" Watkinson knew this to be a lie, but allowed Poundall to continue anyway "I only took the job because we're skint and way behind with the bills. What do I get if I tell you what you want to know?"

"Out of here with your life, Mr Poundall. You are not in a situation conducive to bargaining, and I suggest you place your cards upon the table before my patience runs out. I do have other places to be right now."

"Alright, the man you're looking for is Peter Hoskins. He came to me with a story about some photographs that had been sent to his boss. If it got out that he'd been playing around with the wife of one of his work mates, he'd be for the chop."

"I see. This Peter Hoskins, where exactly does he work?"

"He never told me. Said that was on a need to know basis, and that all I had to do was get in, take the file and get back out. I handed the stuff over to him in Hyde Park the other day."

"Yes, we saw you." Watkinson was genuinely pleased at the look of surprise which appeared on his captive's face. "We even watched you during the break in. Did you really believe that you would be allowed to get out of MI5 without being followed?"

"I never saw anyone following me."

"No, I don't suppose you did. We're rather good at that sort of thing. We know exactly where you live, and the fact that you say you have a family was a very clumsy lie. Now in the light of that, are you happy with the rest of your story? This Peter Hoskins, you wouldn't be sending me off on some wild goose chase, now would you?"

"No, it was definitely him and I'll point him out to you if you let me out of here."

"You're going nowhere until I get what I want Mr Poundall. I think that will be all for now, so enjoy the rest of your stay but if there is anything that you feel you need, just tell one of my agents. They're watching you all the time." He smiled once again and left the room.

Graham Poundall was in a tight corner. Giving up his contact would have put him in the gravest danger once released but naming Peter Hoskins, a man he had never met, could make matters worse. It was a gamble he had to take, after all what could they do to him in here that couldn't just as easily happen outside? The only thing he could do now was to sit and wait.

Once back at his office, George Watkinson played back the taped conversation to Steve Marshall. He sat stoned faced throughout the dialogue and made a series of shorthand notes to which he constantly referred as the conversation progressed. When Poundall identified his contact as Peter Hoskins, Marshall's gaze rose sharply from his notepad and he shook his head at his boss.

"Peter Hoskins? Never! I've known the man for years. He'd never do something like this."

"Hmmm" Watkinson sat back with his hands behind his head "I suppose that's exactly what they said about Burgess, Philby and Maclean, and just look how long Anthony Blunt lay low. However, I do think that Poundall is spinning us a yarn in the hope of getting away so we need to take some action before word gets around that we've got him."

"What do you suggest? I mean we can hardly interview the whole staff, and I assume you think that the mole is someone working in the department itself."

"Well although I agree with you about Hoskins, there's a procedure to go through and we need to be seen to be taking action immediately. Instigate the lock down and tell all staff that they are to remain within the building until further notice. Open up the residential rooms and get enough food and water in for a week. Everyone gets one phone call to next of kin, but apart from that we're all in isolation until I'm satisfied. Make sure that there's a complete roll call after the department is secure and locate anyone not on the register. You'd better get Hoskins up here right away and we'll see him together."

Peter Hoskins had joined MI5 from Special Branch five years previously after a spell with the Metropolitan Police. He was young and enthusiastic, and Watkinson didn't have him down as the kind of individual to become involved in any double dealing. Nevertheless his name had come up in an interrogation session and that was a matter which could not be ignored. The summons to George Watkinson's office came as a complete surprise, and his face bore a worried frown as he knocked upon the door. Inside were the head of the department together with Steve Marshall, his direct superior.

"Take a seat please Peter" Marshall waved at the chair opposite Watkinson's desk "We have one or two things which we need to discuss with you. Do you know of a man by the name of Graham Poundall?"

"He's a burglar." The reply came unhesitatingly from a man who quite clearly had nothing to hide. "I believe his name appears a number of times in our files."

"How well do you know him?"

"Not at all beyond what's in the system. Why, what's happened?"

"Your name has been given to us as someone who has been passing information out of the department, and although there is nothing in your file or any cases that you have been involved in to indicate any wrongdoing, we have a procedure to follow."

"I understand sir." Hoskins was confident in his own position to realise that he was being set up. He also knew that if the information which Marshall had was being taken at all seriously, he would now be in custody rather than facing a series of mild questions.

"Our position is this." Watkinson stepped in "Certain documents were removed from these offices some days ago by Graham Poundall and handed over to another person on the outside. We know who now has them, but what concerns me more is the fact that he managed to gain access to the building with such ease. He had to have been helped by someone on the inside. We need to know who that person is. Poundall has attempted to incriminate you in the hope of gaining his own freedom."

"I see sir, so what do you want from me?"

"A name. Someone with whom you have worked on any cases in the recent past. Someone with a link back to Poundall, and someone who may have mentioned your name to him; he could not have learned it by accident."

"There have only been two cases where that's happened, and Christopher Morse was my partner on both of them. Surely you can't be serious, Chris isn't a double agent."

"With great respect Peter, I have seen operatives come and go over a number of years. Some of them would have sold their grandmothers if they could have got away with it. Never be fooled by what's on the surface. We need to flush out Morse if he is indeed our mole, and you are going to be our bait. There will be a full enquiry into your involvement with a known criminal, and the entire department will informed of the proceedings. Make a show of clearing your desk and you will be accompanied to our holding area pending further action."

"How long for sir?"

"That depends. I am going to release Poundall and see how long it takes him to contact Morse. They won't be able to resist checking each other's story to ensure that we don't catch them out, but I'll be waiting."

Peter left the office accompanied by two of Watkinson's security staff, and silence fell like a wave before him as he passed through his assembled colleagues. Many turned away, other stared at walls or the ceiling, but only one watched with interest as he left the area. Watkinson had homed in on Christopher Morse and didn't miss a single expression on the man's face as he followed Hoskins' progress out of the office and down the stairs to the area euphemistically referred to as 'the flat'. A thin smile flitted briefly across the mole's face and George caught it immediately. The trap was now set and with Poundall as the hare soon to be on the run, it was more than likely that Morse would pursue the man and try to eliminate him.

30

Graham Poundall stepped out of the back of the black saloon and squinted in the bright early morning sunlight. The lack of natural daylight at the place of his incarceration together with the tinted, almost black windows in the rear of the car had left him unprepared for his emergence into the free world once more. Not a word had been said to him throughout the journey save for cursory instructions to get in and get out of the vehicle, and as it pulled away from the kerb at the end of his street he wondered at the speed of his release from what he had come to believe would be a lengthy period of captivity. Watkinson had been careful with everything that he had said to Poundall and had not even turned up to supervise the release. The gamble which the burglar had taken appeared to have worked, but as he strode up the path and entered his front door once again he was completely unaware of the two sets of eyes watching his every move from the back of a parked utility services van fifty yards up the street.

He showered to remove the last vestiges of the smell of the room from himself, and filled the washing machine with all of the clothes which he had worn during his period of stay at the place. After a change of attire and a decent meal, he picked up the telephone and dialled the mobile number which Morse had given to him prior to the break in. An automated message told him that the number which he had dialled could not be recognised and that he should check and try again. Christopher Morse had obviously changed his phone after learning of Poundall's arrest, and the burglar would now be forced to wait for the man to contact him and pay the amount agreed for the completion of the job. It wasn't long before his phone rang.

"Hello."

"Poundall?"

"Yes. Who's this?"

"Morse. We need to meet. Where are you now?"

"Home, they've let me go. What happened?"

"Not sure, but one of our guys has been taken away under armed guard. Was that down to you?"

"Yes, and now that I'm out I'm staying out. What about payment for the rest of the job?"

"That's what I need to see you about. I need to close this matter off, and then we must never meet again. When can you get to Waterloo?"

"In about an hour. Where will you be?"

"In the station buffet. I'll be at the table in the back right hand corner. Be there at eleven and I'll give you what's due to you."

The line went dead. The entire conversation had lasted less than a minute, but other ears had heard it all from the back of the utilities van and arrangements were now in progress for an intercept at the main line station. The van remained in position until Poundall had left the house on his way to the rendezvous, and then pulled away heading for central London. Poundall took the first bus from the end of the street for the thirty minute journey into town and the tube station where he would board the underground for the second leg of the trip. He sat in the upper saloon and had not noticed the figure concealed by other passengers at the rear of the section. Not until the final one had left the top deck did the man make his move. Walking quietly up the central aisle whilst Poundall was staring out of the window, he removed the hypodermic syringe from his pocket, plunged it firmly into the man's right arm and emptied its contents into the muscle. Poundall turned around as the pain hit him, and instinctively grabbed his arm at the point where the needle had penetrated.

"You!"

"Yes Graham. I'm not stupid enough to meet you in a public place when your telephone is very probably bugged by MI5, and where you're going you aren't going to need the rest of the £50,000 either."

"What do you mean?" Poundall had started to become drowsy and was having difficulty focussing his eyes on the figure which was now swaying alarmingly before him. Morse looked at his watch.

"In around three minutes you will be unconscious and anyone getting on the bus will simply think you have fallen asleep. By that time I will be far away, and you will not be discovered until the end of the driver's shift when he has returned to the depot. Goodbye Graham, I wish I could say it's been a pleasure dealing with you."

Morse walked away and Poundall didn't even see him descend the stairs on his way off the bus. He was powerless to move and couldn't draw the attention of anyone sitting downstairs. In the allotted three minutes he had lost consciousness, and within a further five was dead. Morse smiled. With the burglar now out of the way, any link to himself was gone with him, and the balance of the £50,000 could be used for more personal reasons – the principals would never find out. When he considered the fuss at the station when the powers that be found themselves outmanoeuvred, he could barely conceal his delight at having outfoxed the fox. If he had known of the tail placed discreetly in the lower saloon of the London bus he would not have been too pleased with himself. George Watkinson was not a man to put all of his eggs into one basket, and the back up was now following Morse's every move as he crossed the street and hailed a taxi cab. A short radio call had one of the department's teams following behind it in an unmarked car.

The tail tracked Morse to Marble Arch where he left the cab, crossed to Cumberland Gate and entered Hyde Park. Here he lit a cigarette and sat down on one of the benches. It appeared to be the place of choice for those under Watkinson's watchful eye, and an ideal rendezvous spot with a regular flow of pedestrians to disguise any covert activity. An arrest here may pose significant danger to members of the public and with any number of escape routes it was a very difficult place to control. Other security vehicles had joined the tail and all major routes in and out of the park were covered. Watkinson's instructions had been those of a watching brief, and the agents blended in with the public to await developments.

Alan Mason approached the park from Kensington Road and crossed over The Serpentine on Exhibition Road. He sat down at the end of the bench occupied by Morse and took out a newspaper. Using it as a screen they carried on a detailed but brief conversation, and five minutes later left the area in opposite directions. The teams assigned by Watkinson took one target each and followed them out of the park. Now was the time to make the first move in the mopping up routine, and Watkinson issued the intercept command as the two pedestrians made their way back to their points of origin.

Christopher Morse smiled as the familiar figures approached him. He would try to bluff his way out of the trouble which he could see fast coming his way by claiming to be under cover on the instructions of George Watkinson himself. It was a clumsy tactic and cut no ice with the stern faces who took him firmly by the arms and led him to a waiting black saloon car. The arrest was carried out with such precision and speed that it was doubtful if the passing public even noticed its happening. Alan Mason on the other hand, took quite a different stance. His position within the Metropolitan Police had afforded him the security of a respectable and powerful role within law enforcement. He was not about to surrender without some kind of a show of opposition.

"Yes? What is it? What do you want?"

"Alan Mason?" The MI5 agent blocked his way, and Mason could see two others flanking him in anticipation of a flight.

"And if I am?"

"Come with me please sir, there are some questions which we would like to ask you."

"Do you know who you're talking to?"

"Yes sir, but my instructions are to ask that you come along with us, preferably without a struggle."

Mason glanced around, but with no obviously immediate exit route, and faced with three experienced operatives; he reluctantly conceded and accompanied them to a waiting car. All his police training had taught him to identify and take advantage of the smallest slip in an opponent's actions, and when two of the agents had moved to the front of the vehicle, he feigned a stumble as the third one opened the rear door to usher him inside. The man was taken briefly by surprise and a short right hook to the underside of his jaw had him unconscious before he hit the ground. Mason was off and running in an instant, and by the time the other two agents had realised what had happened he had crossed Knightsbridge and was heading for the relative safety of the underground tube station at Hyde Park

Corner. With one agent remaining with the vehicle and a stricken colleague, the third set off in pursuit but was unable to prevent Mason from entering the station where, moments later, he was boarding the northbound train on the Piccadilly line heading for Cockfosters. They had lost him.

31

*T*hat George Watkinson was not pleased with the three agents now before him went without saying, and the dressing down which had just finished had been heard all across the department. Their exit from his office was completed in an atmosphere of tension and complete silence as they made their separate ways to fresh assignments with new partners. He was not a man to tolerate sloppiness and had rotated operatives very successfully in the past. He sent for Steve Marshall and they went from the office to the holding cells where Christopher Morse had been cooling his heels for a number of hours. Again Watkinson's tactic of allowing suspects to stew in their own juices seemed to have paid off, as the renegade agent was on his feet as soon as they entered the room.

"Sit down Morse." He barked out the command and pulled up a couple of chairs to face the mole. "There are a number of things which I will now reveal to you in order that you fully understand the depths of the trouble into which you have descended."

Morse's face was extremely pale. His clumsy bluff had clearly been relayed to Watkinson and he was now at the complete mercy of MI5. He slumped in his chair and took out a packet of cigarettes. Watkinson glared at him and he thought better of it, returning them to his pocket.

"We have been tracking the movements of Graham Poundall and know that you and he were involved in the removal of certain documents from my office a few days ago. Poundall has been found dead on the top deck of a London bus and I am certain that by the time our forensic boys have finished with the body they will have found enough evidence to link you to the killing."

"You can't prove I was responsible for the poisoning." Morse smiled for the first time.

"No-one mentioned poison, Morse. I wonder how you came by that information."

The mole's face fell. He was trapped by a clumsy attempt at cleverness and now felt well and truly cornered.

"We also know that the documents in question are now in the possession of Alan Mason, a man with whom you had a meeting today in Hyde Park and who is currently at large. Unlike you he has escaped us temporarily, but there's nowhere he can run to. Like you, he is under suspicion of murder and a nationwide alert is, as we speak, circulating throughout the media. We will have him in custody within a day or so."

Watkinson rose from his chair at this point and strode slowly and purposefully around the room as Morse absorbed the information. He had done this on many occasions and the resulting pressure on any suspect usually bore fruit very quickly. Morse sat for a while under the gaze of Steve Marshall and shuffled his feet nervously; his hands had begun to sweat and he rubbed them on the legs of his trousers. None of this escaped the eagle eye of the MI5 chief.

"So Morse, what did they offer you?" He rounded sharply on the mole and slammed his hands flat down on the table, causing a loud 'bang' and startling the already jumpy suspect.

"What?" The reply was almost inaudible and Watkinson sat down directly opposite and leaned forwards across his folded arms.

"I said" replied the inquisitor "What did they promise you? Was it the undying thanks of a grateful nation? Was it some elevated position in their idea of a new order? Or was it simply down to money?"

The last question was delivered with something approaching a sneer, and with nothing left of whatever resistance he believed he might have, Morse buried his head in his hands and stared at the table. There was an appreciable pause before he raised his eyes once more to meet those of the now victorious Watkinson.

"It's my mother."

"What about your mother?"

"My parents are both elderly and have no savings. My mother is seriously ill and the only cure is an expensive course of treatment at a Hungarian clinic. I needed the money to pay for the journey to Budapest and the hospital costs."

"And you never, at any time, considered coming to me? What were you thinking of man? You've ruined your career on the word of a man who has no business calling himself a British citizen. Do you really think that any promises made to you would have been honoured?"

Watkinson looked sideways at Steve Marshall who shook his head.

"I had no idea sir." He turned to Morse "Chris, do you know what was in the files which you helped to steal?"

"No sir. I was just instructed to remove them from the office. The envelope containing them was never opened whilst it was in my possession, and I was told to eliminate Poundall as the only witness who could tie any of us to the files."

"You're a murderer" Watkinson stepped in again "And should suffer the full weight of the law in settlement of what you've done. However............"

Morse's face rose from the table where he had allowed it to rest in the face of the accusations from both men. He detected a softening in Watkinson's voice and looked eagerly for the way out of the situation which the man's voice was hinting at.

"There may be a way in which you can still be of use. You will not, of course, be able to remain within the department and there will be a show trial at which you will be found guilty on a charge of causing grievous bodily harm. Nevertheless we may be able to engineer your disappearance within the prison system, and you could re-emerge elsewhere to serve our needs covertly."

"I'll do whatever I can sir." The sentence was delivered almost too quickly and Watkinson's gaze scoured Morse for any hint of a hidden agenda. There was none.

"You'll be working for Steve and will have no contact with any other member of this department. All instructions will come from him, and we will have a tracking device installed beneath your skin to avoid the possibility of detection by any hostile opponent. Is that clear?"

"Yes sir, it is."

Morse was taken back to the holding cell to await whatever fate the justice system sought to mete out to him, and Watkinson turned to Marshall.

"Steve, I want Mason picked up and back here as soon as possible. Put all available resources on it and bully New Scotland Yard into giving you their full attention. It's one of theirs we're after and he's a fugitive from a murder charge. Throw the name of Graham Poundall at them and say that we have forensic evidence which places him at the scene."

With two of the three perpetrators of the MI5 break in now eliminated and the third surely only a matter of hours away from custody, George Watkinson was on the verge of exposing the biggest scandal to assail the British public since the Profumo affair in 1962. He reached inside the right hand drawer of his new desk and pulled out the now familiar file of documents. He sat back in his chair as he leafed through their contents and shook his head in wonderment at the names within the dossiers. There were a couple of dozen individuals who had escaped the allied forces in 1945 and made their way to Britain under a sophisticated set of alternative identities. Many of them, Watkinson was sure, would now be dead but three or four of those before him were certainly still living in comparative comfort in Britain's leafy suburbia.

Their casually assumed peace and quiet was to be unceremoniously shattered very soon, and those to whom they had passed on their mantles of the Master Race would be weeded out and treated to the civilised world's closest comparison to that barbarity visited upon their hapless victims over forty years ago. He closed the files and placed them in a new, concealed safe behind the panelling of his office. Mason was not the man at the top of the pyramid nor, he suspected was the Prime minister's private secretary but it would not need too many cages to be rattled before the rest of the rats came scurrying out of the woodwork. The time was now; there would be no better opportunity to put this entire matter away for good. If they missed just one of those responsible for the perpetuation of the organisation the lives of Tom Skerritt and Watkinson's two agents would have been given in vain.

32

Alan Mason had been on the run for over a week since his escape from the clutches of the agents sent to apprehend him; his appearance during that time had changed dramatically from that of the smartly dressed police officer. Having exchanged clothing with a homeless man and remained unshaven in the intervening period, it was safe to say that none of his colleagues at the Met would have recognised him let alone any of Watkinson's operatives. In his new guise as one of the tramps who routinely patrol the streets of the capital, he had made his way to New Scotland Yard in the hope of somehow gaining access to his office and the mobile phone with which he could summon those within the organisation who could help. He found the place staked out by an obvious presence of two of Watkinson's teams of agents, and turned back the way he had come. His only other alternative was to walk the six miles across London to his home and hide there.

Here too he encountered a surveillance squad, and it seemed as though MI5 had all eyes and ears out searching for him. He returned to the hostel where he had been spending the intervening time amongst the rest of the capital city's unfortunates, and lay on the crude cot provided by a charitable organisation for such as him. As the day wore on he began to appreciate the lot of the army of vagrants wandering aimlessly around the streets each day, but shook himself out of this lethargy when an idea occurred to him. He took his notebook from the inside pocket of the tattered old raincoat he had acquired from a grateful tramp in exchange for his own quality clothing. There in the index was the address of Julie and Doug Martin, the couple who first set the whole matter of the files in motion. He could get up to Solihull by travelling with a group of itinerants using empty carriages on the goods trains which left London each day for Birmingham and the West Midlands. It should be quite easy to track them down once he had left the train before it entered New Street.

Turning over on the dingy bed, Mason shut his eyes in preparation for the journey on the following day, and smiled for the first time in over a week as he drifted off to sleep. He was awake and out of the hostel very early the next morning heading for the staging area where the rest of the day's travellers were accustomed to gather. He doubted whether anyone would be looking for him at this place, and boarded an empty cattle truck along with a dozen or more individuals of similar intent to him. As journeys went it was not an unpleasant one, and the camaraderie amongst the group lightened his spirits as they shared amongst themselves what meagre items of food and drink they possessed. The train arrived at New Street shortly before ten o'clock and amidst a hasty scramble to avoid the railway police they all disembarked and disappeared across the sidings outside the main terminal.

Mason had to find a map of the city and its outlying areas. He would have to walk – no-one in their right mind was going to offer him a lift. Passing a newsagents shop he noticed a rack of street maps outside the front door, and taking one carefully from the display he was able to walk away without anyone noticing what he had done. Finding a park bench he spread out the map, and locating the street listed in his notebook calculated that he had a distance of around three miles to walk. Without wishing to draw attention to himself, and adopting the shuffling gait of the typical vagrant, it would take him approximately an hour to make the trip. Reaching into his pocket he pulled out the rest of the crust which he had concealed from the others in the travelling group and ate it hungrily. Water from the tap of a public toilet washed it down, much to his distaste and with a deep breath he started out on the trek across the city.

Although his face and a description of his attire had been plastered all across the media for a week, Alan Mason was confident that he would remain untroubled by the public or the police, and so it proved as he neared the area of Solihull which was his destination.

He checked his pockets. The gun was still there, loaded and ready for the time coming very soon when he was sure that it would be needed. Turning into the street where the Martins lived, he rechecked the house number in his notebook and shuffled unsteadily up the path and round the side of the house to the back door – no experienced tramp ever used the front, it left him too exposed to nosey neighbours. He glanced around the well-kept garden and envied the family and their anonymity. A sharp rap at the door brought the sound of footsteps through the kitchen. Julie Martin opened the door with a smile on her face which died the minute she saw the dirty figure before her. She frowned and tried to look intimidating.

"Yes, what do you want?"

"Spare some food and a drink missus." Mason preened himself at the act which he put on. A week's growth of untidy beard had leant him an altogether unsavoury appearance.

"You'll go away if I do?" Anxious to free herself from the disgusting figure in her garden, she stopped the door with the toe of her foot, talking only through the narrow gap between it and the post.

"'Course I will missus." He leered as if to lend weight to his appearance.

"Wait there." She closed the door and went to one of the cupboards. Mason stepped inside the kitchen. Julie dropped the plate she was holding when he appeared beside her as she turned around. She screamed, but with no-one else in the house and all neighbours out of earshot it was only a reflex reaction.

"Sit down and listen!" Mason produced the hand gun and waved her towards an empty chair. His voice had resumed it normal tone and pitch, and Julie stared open-mouthed at the transformation.

"Who are you?" Shakily she moved to keep the table between them and pulled out one of the kitchen chairs.

"I said shut up! Your only chance of getting out of this alive is by listening to me and doing exactly what I say, understand?"

"Yes." The reply was almost inaudible and she looked around for some means of defending herself. Mason spotted it right away.

"Don't even think about it. When's that husband of yours due home, and what about your kids?"

"Doug finishes work about now, and the children are at his parents' this week. He'll be home very soon." She tried to sound brave and defiant, as if Doug would ride in like some white knight and rescue her.

"Right, we'll just sit and wait for him then. Get me a drink and don't do anything stupid, I've got nothing to lose by using this thing." He waved the gun at her.

One further matter to take care of; he picked up the Martins' telephone and dialled a number of his own. The voice at the other end was sharp and to the point.

"Yes, who is this?"

"Mason."

"Good God! Where the hell are you man? Don't you know there's a manhunt on for you? What did you do?"

"Never mind all that. Trace this number and get some of your men up here. I'm in a tight corner with MI5 on the way. Once I get out of the place you can pick me up and I'll need somewhere to hide."

"Out of the question. I shouldn't even be talking to you any more. MI5 have got the entire police force on the case. You don't stand a chance of getting away. Don't ring this number again."

The line went dead and Mason cursed. With his last escape route now closed the gun was his only possible bargaining chip. True to his perfect timing, Doug Martin chose that moment to breeze in through the front door with his usual announcement that he was home. The silence puzzled him and hanging up his coat, he looked in the lounge. Strange; Julie was normally in there reading a magazine and drinking one of the two coffees which were always ready for this time of day. He frowned, shrugged his shoulders and made for the kitchen; perhaps she was in the garden talking to Gloria from next door. Pushing open the door he smiled automatically when he saw Julie sitting at the table, but it faded away when he saw the look on her face. The muzzle of the gun now pressed into the back of his neck killed all sense of pleasure at coming home, and he turned slowly at the gunman's command to face him.

"Who the hell are you?" Doug spat the words out at the derelict standing before him, but followed the waving gun to another of the kitchen chairs where he sat down. "You Ok, Jules?" He held his wife's hand and tried to put Mason out of his mind for a moment.

152

"There's no point in keeping it secret now." Mason sat down at the opposite end of the table and far away from any possible attempt to wrench the gun away from him. "My name is Alan Mason, and until very recently I was a senior policeman at New Scotland Yard but the two of you now see before you the result of all your meddling in things which you don't understand."

"Meddling?" Then Doug suddenly realised what had happened. "You're after the files aren't you? What's the matter, Watkinson take them away from you?" The attempt at sarcasm riled Mason and his face turned white with rage. In any one-to-one situation Doug could easily have disarmed the man who was smaller than him and appeared to be of slight build, but the gun more then evened things up in Mason's favour, and he thought better of any further insults. "What is it that you want from us?"

"A way out of the country with one of you as a hostage. If you're familiar with George Watkinson, get on the phone to him and tell him that I'm here. I want transport and a plane out of the country within twenty-four hours, Understand?"

They all moved to the lounge where Martin made the call to the mobile number Watkinson had given him up in Morecambe. The conversation was brief and once over, Mason sat facing the wide bay window with the two of them before him. From this position he would be able to see all movement outside the house and there would be no possibility of a surprise attack from behind. It was now a case of wait and see; he knew that Watkinson would not take the situation lying down but he held all the cards at present.

33

Watkinson stepped out of the police helicopter at Birmingham Airport. All flights had been suspended to give them a clear run into the area and the black Mercedes sent to meet him sped away towards Solihull with a team of agents following on behind in another vehicle. The local Chief Constable was beside him, and a tactical firearms squad had been assembled and sent to the Martins' address. They arrived there twenty minutes later to find the entire street cleared of occupants and sealed off at either end. Armoured police vans littered the area, and with sets of officers brandishing side arms it was clear that Mason would not be leaving the area a free man. Watkinson surveyed the area and looked across the street to the properties directly opposite the Martins' address.

"Men in position?" He asked the inspector in charge.

"Yes sir. Rifles in both of the upstairs windows facing the property in question and two more covering the rear; we're in radio contact and they'll fire on your command."

"Good men?"

"The best. All ex-army snipers. High velocity weapons with telescopic sights and laser targeting. If the red light touches the target it's as good as hit."

"Excellent. Any requests coming out of the house?"

"Just one call once we set up the communications link, and it was a male asking if you were here yet. Sounded impatient."

"Better give him a call then. Where's the incident trailer."

They walked down the street and past the Martins' house to a large mobile headquarters the size of a Winnebago. Watkinson stepped inside to hear the telephone already blaring out.

"Looks like you're expected sir." The sergeant handed Watkinson the microphone and headphones, and switched on the recording device.

Watkinson let the call ring a little longer before flicking the switch to receive the transmission.

"George Watkinson."

"Took your time didn't you? I've got the Martins at the end of a gun in here, and their lives depend on you and your men following my instructions to the letter, clear?"

"As crystal. What is it that you want Mr Mason? You surely don't think that this little drama of yours is going to get you a ticket out of here."

"If it doesn't I'm taking these two with me, so make your mind up what you're going to do about it and don't keep me waiting. I'll give you twenty-four hours to come up with some transport or one of them dies and I don't much care which it is."

The line went dead and George Watkinson's stepped out of the van, a grave and thoughtful look on his face. It was now clear that any attempt to storm the property with Mason in control would result in tragedy for the Martin family, and that was to be avoided at all costs. There was no way out of the situation for the ex-policeman, and the only question remaining was whether to take him down permanently or try to incapacitate him in some way and force an entry whilst he was down. He called both the inspector and the Chief Constable to a meeting and outlined an idea to them.

"We need to use one of the snipers to wound Mason so that we can get into the house. Make it clear to your shooters that I want the man alive, and position a tactical squad close to all the doors so that we can get in as soon as he's hit. There'll be no margin for error."

With four rifles trained on the Martin house, all windows and doors were covered. Each sniper was given a call signal with Watkinson on the other end of a radio link co-ordinating the operation. Mason and the Martins remained in the lounge area for some time, giving the rifleman located in the front room of the house directly opposite the best shot. He tracked Mason's every move around the room, keeping him continually in the gun sights. Reports were radioed to Watkinson at ten minute intervals concerning the current status of the situation. Alan Mason was acutely aware of his vulnerability, but needed the lounge curtains open to keep a watch on developments outside. Nevertheless he had to keep ahead of the game, and suddenly moved all three of them to the kitchen without warning. A rash of calls flashed across the radio link informing Watkinson of the change in the situation.

With the hours passing, dusk was starting to fall and the odds were rapidly changing to favour the firearms teams trained upon the house. Watkinson visited each position in turn to assess the snipers' chances of a hit. All were on high alert, with the rear sniper located on the roof of a local garage. This position was his final call and the rifleman was lying flat across the roof some fifty yards from the house. He looked around as Watkinson's head appeared above the guttering behind him and gave the 'thumbs up' signal that he was ready to go. Watkinson waved and came back down the ladder. Terry Collins turned back to his target and smiled. This would be his fifth kill after Tom Skerritt, Miranda Farnley and the two MI5 agents, and one which he would have no trouble explaining away. The order had been issued to shoot but not to kill, but if Mason made an unexpected move at the last minute the shot may well prove to be fatal. There was no-one else covering his line of sight at the rear of the premises and with his career in the force unblemished there would be no doubting his word. He settled down to wait.

Inside the house, Doug Martin was becoming impatient at the lack of activity in the street and had tried to bait Mason into making a move on several occasions, but the man wouldn't bite. He knew that he might be able to disarm him if he could only get close, but the distance between them remained just enough to provide the man with a clear shot. He also had Julie to think about and Mason was nearer to her than he was himself; he would have to wait until fatigue began to set in -- surely the man would not be able to remain awake until the morning. The next few hours were tense within the Martin home but Doug and Julie were able to snatch a few brief hours sleep. A noise at the back door caused Doug to stir and he noticed immediately that Mason was not in the room. Removing his shoes to avoid alerting the man he crept towards the lighted kitchen to see him staring out into the pre-dawn darkness, clearly looking for some sign of an attempt to access the property.

Deciding that this was probably going to be his only chance of regaining control of his own home, Doug made his play. Mason caught sight of the movement by the lounge door as he turned back into the kitchen. From that point, everything seemed to move in slow motion. Mason had pocketed the revolver and was now reaching into his coat to retrieve it as his captive rushed him from the other side of the room. The gun was out as Doug hit him with the full force of a blow aimed at the side of his head. It never made full contact as Mason dodged to one side, and they became locked in a hand-to-hand struggle for the weapon. A shot rang out as their hands closed around it and a bullet shattered the back door glass panel.

On the garage roof, fifty yards away, Terry Collins had been watching Mason's movements since his entrance into the kitchen, and reports in to Watkinson had resulted in an instruction to incapacitate the man as a preliminary to a full attack on the house from all sides. The struggle in the kitchen changed all that, and it became a priority to ensure the safety of the Martins. Squinting down the telescopic sight, Collins turned on the laser targeting mechanism and homed in on the moving figures in the lighted room. For a marksman such as he was, it would have been a bread and butter shot to wound Mason without causing any harm to Doug Martin, but instructions from his principals in London had been quite clear; Mason was to be eliminated and any danger of his revealing sensitive information removed forever.

He waited and waited for the perfect opportunity as the struggle continued in the house. Julie Martin's appearance at the lounge doorway lent another dimension to the situation, and Watkinson's voice over the earpiece radio barked out the command to take the shot. Collins did just that, and a single cartridge case spun back over his head as the high velocity bullet flashed with unerring accuracy towards the open kitchen door. It entered just below the lintel, shattering the glass panel above the door and pierced Mason's skull just below the right ear. He was dead before he hit the floor as his skull exploded with the impact. Blood and brain tissue splattered all over the kitchen as Doug Martin reeled backwards under the weight of Mason's body. Julie had stood transfixed in silence as the scene unfolded before her, but now screamed in panic as the room was flooded with heavily armed, black-clad 'troops' bellowing out instructions to the survivors.

157

On the garage roof, Terry Collins was clearing up his position in preparation for the usual debriefing. He was unconcerned at the outcome of the siege; he had followed instructions and Mason's last move had taken him into an unforeseen position, resulting in a fatality instead of the intended wounding. He would be questioned of course, but things like this had been happening since the seventies and he had, after all, ensured the safety of two innocent members of the public. The men in London would be very pleased with his work today and his position as an agent within the Metropolitan Police was assured for another day.

34

*A*t the first sound of the pistol shot Watkinson moved all units into final positions ready for the assault on the front of the house, and Collins' report on the activity in the kitchen forced his hand. He hadn't expected the scene of carnage as he stepped into the rear of the house and his first concern was for the Martins. Julie was crouched on the floor with Doug in her arms. He was bleeding from a cut to the head where shards of glass from the doorway had hit him as he turned, with the body of Mason, towards the ground. It looked much worse than it was but the man was clearly in a state of shock. Arriving paramedics not surprisingly pronounced Mason dead at the scene and were now attending to Doug. Julie stood up as they treated her husband and turned into Watkinson's arms as he arrived.

"George! Thank you, oh thank you. You saved our lives. He was going to kill us."

"I know Julie, are you sure you're unhurt?"

"I'm alright, just a little shaken but what about Doug?"

Watkinson looked down at the paramedics and got a 'thumbs up' signal. The two of them would be taken in to the nearest hospital for a check up, but the kitchen would need considerable attention before it was fit for use again.

With Mason now dead the chances of getting to the root of his organisation seemed to have vanished, and Watkinson privately cursed his luck. He had given clear instructions that the man was to be taken alive and yet circumstances appeared to have conspired to frustrate all his efforts once again. The sniper, Collins, was an experienced copper and on the face of it Watkinson had no reason to doubt the man's word that Doug Martin's life had been in imminent danger. Nevertheless he couldn't shake off the nagging feeling that there was more to the matter than a simple case of protecting an innocent member of the public. Certainly silencing Mason would only work in favour of the organisation which MI5 were trying to expose.

A call to Steve Marshall back in London would have all Collins' records, personal and professional, available for him upon his return. The two of them would go through the whole lot with a fine toothed comb if only to allay any suspicion that yet another force was operating within the system and contrary to their objectives. Until then the Martins were his main concern; they had put themselves firmly in the firing line for a cause which neither of them fully understood and for which they were not expecting any recompense. Watkinson would see to it that neither of them went unrewarded for the danger which they had inflicted upon themselves. With no further reason to remain, he left the scene to the clear up squad, held a short meeting with the Inspector and Chief Constable and made his way back to the car which had brought him from the airport.

At a separate debriefing meeting further down the street, Terry Collins had kept a wary eye on George Watkinson. Whilst he was sure that his version of today's events would not be challenged, it was far from certain that the man would not try to link him with the deaths of Skerritt and the Farnley woman. He could not be absolutely sure that no evidence had been left at either site which could be used to connect him with the killings but any potential attack on the head of an organisation like MI5 was beyond his capabilities.

Steve Marshall, anticipating Watkinson's needs for their meeting, had dug out the case details on the killings of Tom Skerritt and Miranda Farnley. It had only been four years since Colin Pitchfork had been convicted of murder based on the new technique of DNA fingerprinting. Evidence gathered from both of their crime scenes had been sent back to the lab for comparison with a number of profiles from the police files; one of them was that of Terry Collins. Watkinson's arrival back at the office coincided exactly with the delivery of the results of the comparisons, but for the moment he kept it back as his boss focussed on the information which he had requested. Marshall came back from the coffee machine with two cups to find Watkinson staring at the documents before him. He flicked impatiently through the sheets, looking for evidence of unexplained absences from work corresponding with the dates and times of the deaths of Skerritt and Farnley.

"Yes!" The exclamation, though not unexpected by Steve since he had seen the same information some hours before, still caused him surprise. "Look, two periods of off-duty time matching our killings."

"Yes sir, but that's not enough on its own, he would simply say that he was at home at the time. We would have to have something pretty damning, like an eye witness statement, to bring him in on a charge."

"You're right, damn it!" Watkinson leaned back in his chair and stared out of the window. "We need something concrete to tie him to at least one of the murders."

"Like this?" Marshall had chosen his moment perfectly, and Watkinson spun round from the window.

"What's that?"

"Remember about four years back? Late January 1988, a Leicestershire baker named Colin Pitchfork was convicted of murder on the basis of DNA fingerprinting. It's still a fairly new technique, but I've had evidence re-examined from both our scenes."

"And...............?"

"We have a match to some hair samples found in the cottage in Morecambe where Tom Skerritt was shot. It places Terry Collins at the scene. Now what could he possibly be doing up there when he's based down in London?"

"You sure of this?"

"Absoltuely. I had the lab run his samples two more times after the original one came back as positive. We have him at the scene, and a partial fingerprint on Skerritt's mobile came back as a 60% match, not enough on its own to enable us to charge him, but when you put it together with the DNA evidence I'd say that he's going to have trouble getting out of this one."

Terry Collins had arrived home at the end of his shift and was in the shower when the hammering at his front door had him descending the stairs dressed only in a bath sheet. He opened the door to be faced with armed police in riot gear; he counted at least six as he was forced back into the house.

"Terry Collins?" The sergeant in charge demanded an answer.

"Yes. What's this all about? What the hell do you think you're doing?"

"Get dressed and come with us. Jones, Marsh, go upstairs with him and watch him like a hawk. I want him back down here in five minutes."

Steve Marshall had followed them into the house and was now co-ordinating a search of the premises and the removal of any evidence. By the time they had finished and secured the property, two vans were heading back to MI5 filled with property from the house. With the site now taped off and under armed guard, he made his own way back to the office with the now fully dressed Terry Collins handcuffed and in the car beside him.

George Watkinson left Collins to sweat it out for two days before interviewing him. During that time all the items removed from his home had been examined in minute detail. That property included a handgun and silencer which had been sent to ballistics for tests against the bullets removed from Miranda Farnley, Tom Skerritt and Madeline Fretwell. The results of those tests were now on the desk in front of him, and he pushed the folder across it to Steve Marshall.

"Perfect matches in every case. The silencer left unique striations on the bullets and there's no doubt that it was the weapon used in each of the cases. If the DNA evidence doesn't convict him this certainly will. Let's get him in and finish the job."

Terry Collins presented a pathetic figure of a man when compared to the self-assured sniper of a mere few days ago. He had been given no information of any charges and had not been allowed to see anyone outside the department. His initial clamouring for legal representation had become very muted when the realisation finally dawned upon him that the gun found at his home would be enough on its own to tie him to at least two killings. He sat before George Watkinson and stared at the floor, resigned to his fate and totally submissive.

"Collins!" The words caused him to start, and Watkinson noticed that his clothing was bathed in perspiration. His head snapped upwards to meet his interrogator's gaze.

"Yes?" The words were whispered and he was beginning to shake. He clasped his hands in an attempt to brace himself for the inevitable grilling.

"Been a very naughty boy, haven't we?" Words spoken very softly, almost considerately by Watkinson in another twist to his technique of keeping suspects off guard.

"What?" Collins' confusion at the change in tack was now complete and it was Marshall who moved in for the kill.

"Terry, why don't you tell us all about Alan Mason? We know that you've been working under cover for him, and we've got enough evidence to convict you on two counts of murder. If you've been working for some foreign organisation as well, you'll never see the outside of a prison cell again."

"I'm just someone he used to get jobs done. I was never a part of his organisation."

"Not good enough! You're a murderer, and one used by a fascist organisation for its own ends. Do you think that that kind of excuse will help you any more than it did the SS when the Nazis finally fell at the end of 1945?"

With nowhere to go and no way out of the situation, Terry Collins crumbled under the pressure. His testimony over the next three days was enough to lead Watkinson to a series of names forming the pyramid of power within a structure whose sole intent was to be the suppression of democracy within Britain. How close they had come to achieving those aims had not become totally apparent to the head of MI5 until now, and the disclosure of Collins and the trail they were going to lead him down sent a shiver down his spine.

35

*R*oger and Madeline Fretwell had watched the developments surrounding the siege at Solihull with an intense fascination. They had, on Watkinson's advice moved back to the former Colson family home in Cleethorpes rather than encounter a host of awkward questions back in Tewkesbury. Madeline now accepted that the period of their lives spent in the idyllic surroundings of the River Avon was over, and that she, at least, was back where she truly belonged. The house brought back many memories of childhood and her stern but loving father, and with the rambling property filled with the sound of her son Brian and his family she was happier than she had been for some time.

She and Roger had placed flowers on the grave of Tom Skerritt the week after their return to the east coast, and it was then that they bumped into Bert Peterson. Bert had taken the news of Tom's death very hard; the man had been his oldest friend and with no-one now to share recollections of their time in the army he had become rather reclusive despite the attentions of his daughter. The Fretwells gave him a new lease of life, and he and Roger shared a set of fresh memories of past times in the armed forces. Inevitably their conversations came around to the subject of the papers which Roger had brought back from Germany at the end of the war, and today they were mulling over the events of the past fortnight and the series of arrests which had hit the news headlines.

George Watkinson had been very active after the confession obtained from Terry Collins. The man had supplied a list of contacts within the police and civil service, and although the individuals concerned were not at a high enough level in themselves to affect the policy of the organisation, the ripples they caused had a dramatic effect further up the pyramid. A 'leaked' document had appeared in one of the weekend tabloids noted for its exposés, and Watkinson had watched with intense interest as the rest of the media homed in on the biggest scandal to hit Britain for over thirty years. To have compared the mass exodus of numbers of high profile public figures to rats leaving a doomed ship would have been an understatement and MI5 were able to cherry pick those responsible for the running of the organisation as their heads appeared above the public parapet.

"How many more do you think there are?" Madeline had emerged from the kitchen carrying a tray laden with tea and cakes.

"Hard to say" replied Bert "I was never that involved in the intricate stuff that Tom was into. He only used me when he needed something – like the letter in the Martins' caravan."

"That last batch caused a right stir in the city by all accounts." Roger Fretwell put his newspaper down on the table and tapped an article in the business section of the Telegraph.

"What will happen to the people that George Watkinson has arrested?" Madeline poured out the tea and sat down next to her husband.

"If it were me" Bert continued "I'd throw the book at all of them. Lock the lot up and then forget where the key was. It was lucky you brought those brief cases back with you Roger. Heaven only knows what might have happened if they'd got into the wrong hands. Was Bormann ever found?"

"Not as far as I can tell." Roger laughed "D'you know, I might have been the last person to catch sight of the man. There have been reported sightings of him over the years, but nothing confirmed as concrete. It doesn't matter any more, our part in it is over. It's all down to George Watkinson now."

Watkinson was, at that very moment, knocking on the last of a series of doors. In a leafy Berkshire village amid the rural beauty of Britain's well-heeled class, he had strolled up the paved path which curled its way through a large well-stocked garden. This one he had left to the very end and it would give him a sense of immense pleasure to personally arrest the man who was second in command in the hierarchy of the organisation. There would, inevitably, be numbers of 'foot soldiers' who would escape the tightening net and that was unavoidable, but this one was a major prize. The door opened and a man in his late fifties stood facing Watkinson. His hair was steely grey and he had the bearing of someone who had become accustomed to the trappings of power during his rise to the top of the civil service.

"Good morning George, been expecting you. Come in."

"Marcus" said Watkinson and followed the man into an oak panelled study where an open fire was crackling away. They sat down in a pair of Chesterfields and Marcus Timson poured out two measures of single malt.

"Your health." Timson raised his glass, and Watkinson's gaze was drawn to the service revolver on the bureau in the corner. He nodded in its direction.

"Not thinking of doing anything silly are we?"

"It crossed my mind. When Margaret died some years ago the job was the only thing I had left, and that now appears to be a thing of the past. Perhaps you'd better take it along with you."

"It's over, Marcus. We've got the files and everyone mentioned in them is either dead or in custody along with all those who joined the organisation's power base over the years."

Timson stared out of the window and shook his head. His face suddenly bore all the traces of a man who had lost the will to continue and Watkinson pocketed the revolver in case he changed his mind.

"You have to come along with us now. I have a car waiting outside and we'll be in London within the hour. There's just one more to round up and I'll need his name from you. No-one else seems to know who he is."

"In that case my friend, you're out of luck. I'll never reveal his identity to you, and there really isn't anything that you can do to me now which would persuade me to change my mind."

Watkinson nodded. He knew that this last card would be denied him and he really hadn't tried too hard to get the information out of Marcus Timson. Nevertheless with the head of the organisation still at large he could never be truly certain that its entire structure had been eliminated.

36

*I*n a boardroom somewhere in the Midlands, what remained of the organisation was now seated around a nondescript table in an anonymous building on an industrial estate. The six there were all that was left of the power structure which had been so carefully and meticulously laid down since the early fifties. Those originally involved in the early days were now no longer alive, but sons and daughters had continued the work which had been so efficiently destroyed by the very system which had been targeted to underpin their vision of the future. A seventh figure entered the room and their collective gaze homed in on him as all conversation abruptly ceased.

Since the meeting in Marcus Timson's office in Whitehall the man had kept a low profile, watching events unfold with an increasing sense of frustration. He had made his feelings known to Marcus on a number of occasions, but the radical views he expressed on the elimination of George Watkinson had been silenced by those present as too extreme. That he had been proven to be right was, in his mind, a complete vindication of the way in which he had wanted the organisation to proceed. Timson's weakness had cost them all dearly and it was now down to him to rescue what was left and rebuild.

"What are your instructions sir?" A fresh-faced young woman in her early twenties interrupted the expectant silence in the room. The man looked up.

"The six of you are going to help me to rebuild what is left of the plan. Your existing positions within the organisation have, until now, been at a fairly junior level. It's time to take a step up. There's very little to work with at present, but I still have influence in a number of circles, and my second in command is the only man who can identify me."

"What if he talks?" A young man this time, eerily reminiscent of the photographs which had been taken of the Hitler Youth during the early days of the Third Reich.

"I can assure you that there is no danger of that, and because I am safe so are all of you. There is nothing that the security forces can do to him; he is terminally ill and has only a few months to live."

"What next then?" He pushed for an answer, almost over keen to get on with the job.

"It is going to be a long and difficult road. We will simply start all over again; just because Britain has rejected us once does not mean that it does not need us. No-one likes taking unpleasant medicine, but we will prevail in the end. You all need to go back to your normal lives and wait for the call. It will come, maybe not soon, but it will. I will contact each of you when the time is right, but under no circumstances should any of you attempt to contact me."

The meeting broke up on this sombre note, and without another word to each other the assembled six made their separate ways back to their homes. Now alone in the office of the company which had funded so much of the operations down the years, he stared out of the window and watched as each of them drove away. This was not the end, and if George Watkinson believed anything other than that he was a fool. The knock at the door brought him out of his reverie.

"Come in." A tall, suited figure entered the room and sat down uninvited. "Martin, I have a job for you." An envelope appeared from the drawer of a desk and slid across the table.

"This is the one. I want it done as soon as possible. Half the fee is already in your bank account and the balance will be paid upon proof of completion. When it's over, disappear and do not try to contact me. Fail me and you will regret it, clear?"

"Clear."

He opened the envelope and spilled out the contents. Detailed notes of the target's location and a schedule of movements were laid out on two sides of A4 paper. A colour photograph was paper clipped to the top of the first page. The face staring out at the assassin was that of George Watkinson. The gunman raised his eyebrows and looked up.

"Now do you understand why this is the final job?"

"Yes, and what if I'm caught?"

"Keep your mouth shut or keep looking over your shoulder for the rest of your life. Fail and I will find you."

He nodded. This was the way it had always been. Leaving the building he returned home to plan out the last hours of George Watkinson's life and the most appropriate way of disposing of him. It would not be easy; people like Watkinson were usually heavily protected in their professional capacity and even at home it was always possible that, like Prime Ministers, they enjoyed the security of a bodyguard and they normally shot first and asked questions later. No, it would take something extra special to finish this job, and it was not a matter to be rushed into.

The array of weaponry at his disposal was impressive. He had operated in a number of countries and had used everything from a sniper's rifle to poison. The armoury was illegal of course, but then again the law only punished those who got caught, and he had been in this line of work for sufficient time to know the ins and outs of law breaking. He would not be caught, of that he was certain.

37

Marcus Timson had been true to his word and had not betrayed the name of the number one in the organisation. George Watkinson had been aware that the man's health was not what it had been by the look upon his face at the arrest and now, one month later was standing at his graveside after the funeral. His illness had been a very aggressive one and he was in considerable pain at the end. Still, with no deathbed revelations, MI5 were left to mop up the remainder of the case without accounting for all of the hierarchy. Security around all the top brass had been tightened during the immediate aftermath of the arrests, and everyone was well aware of the dangers of reprisals. A number of false alarms had triggered the detainment of what turned out to be unfortunate innocent bystanders, as a form of paranoia set in.

That had been some months ago now, and with no other apparent threats to those in positions of power, a period of relative calm had set in with security being wound down from its 'red' status. This was just the kind of easing which the assassin had been waiting for. He had been watching for some time in anticipation of gaps in the security surrounding Watkinson, and had even considered taking out some minor figure in attempt to draw him out. That no longer appeared to be necessary, and with his ability to blend into the background he was free to come and go very much as he pleased around Whitehall where George had been spending a considerable amount of time briefing the cabinet.

He still believed that any attack in the capital was doomed to either failure or his capture, and centred his attention on the Watkinson home in Surrey as the preferable alternative. He had rented a property in the neighbouring village, giving him ample scope for observing his target without raising any alarms. The bodyguard assigned to protect Watkinson was ever present and any close quarter assault therefore impossible without his being apprehended, and the man at the top had made it clear as to the penalties for failure at that level.

The Watkinson house backed on to open fields which were attached to a neighbouring farm, and a series of outlying buildings provided good cover for any surveillance prior to the job. The rear of the property, apart from the halogen floodlights which lit up a patio area usually reserved for family barbeques, was pitch black for most of the darkness hours, and his camouflaged body suit and hood would conceal him perfectly in the undergrowth. A security check was carried out each evening before the property was locked, but the winding down of the alert status had caused the guard to become less than meticulous in his duties. The random timing had now slipped and for convenience it was carried out at the same time each night. A clear window of opportunity was thus presented and it really was too good to miss.

The only remaining consideration was therefore to fix a date and time. The schedule of movements supplied by the client had proved invaluable for tracking Watkinson's regular habits, and with Sunday seeming to be the time of least activity in the village this proved to be the most suitable day for the job. He rested for the whole of the previous week and changed his active hours to fit the needs of a night shift task. When the day selected arrived he was fully prepared and focussed. A two mile hike across open fields from the neighbouring village found him in position at the back of the house. He had set up a firing position for his rifle on an oak tree on the edge of the farm field and now made final preparations for the shot. Test sweeps across the back of the house using the night vision sight had located several figures moving from the lounge to the kitchen and it took a while to discern that of George Watkinson from the rest. As far as he could ascertain, six people were present in the house, and assuming that three of them were Watkinson, his wife and the bodyguard the rest would have to be neighbours round for the evening.

Suddenly the back door opened, spilling a beam of light out on to the back garden and there, caught in the glow was his target. A glance down the sight confirmed the target's identity, but with no bullet yet loaded this window of opportunity would have to be allowed to pass. The figure glanced around the garden, a cat came running in from the undergrowth and the door closed again. With time now on his hands, Martin set about preparing his mode of escape. The initial hit was certain to arouse the guard in the house and the area would be swarming with police in no time. Carefully treading down a path through the grass to a line of hedge some distance away he made that appear as his route away from the site. Time spent in Armagh during the troubles had taught him a number of techniques in concealment, and using material from the surrounding area he had built himself a 'hide' in the undergrowth. The place seemed so natural that he had, on coming back to it, been initially unable to locate the position. He was now ready.

Watkinson's foray into the back garden in search of the cat had given him the chance to stand and listen for any tell-tale signs of danger. Unlike his counterparts in the regular police force he was not convinced about the reduced need for security, and he had remained on alert for anything which might indicate the slightest danger. His pause at the door was the result of an almost indiscernible flicker of light beyond the boundary of the garden some fifty yards away. The sniper was not to know it, but in that instance his position was compromised and with Watkinson closing the door behind him as he returned inside, he assumed that all was well. The kitchen light went out and the occupants of the house retired to the front of the property. Watkinson picked up the telephone.

"Steve? Get down here as soon as you can and bring a tactical team with you. I've got a sniper at the back of the house and we need him alive."

"Ok, how long do we have until he moves on?"

"All the time you need. He's here until I'm dead and as long as we keep him interested he's not likely to suspect anything."

"We'll be there in an hour. No sirens I assume?"

"Very funny. Just get here and keep quiet."

Watkinson looked at his watch. Just before ten, and with the man outside probably on a different clock to the rest of them it should be possible to keep him on his toes until the team arrived. Along with the security guard, he set up a series of manoeuvring in and out of the kitchen and garden area to arouse interest without exposing anyone to danger. He hated bullet-proof vests but now insisted that all the occupants of the house wear one for the evening. Over the course of the next hour or so the sniper was subjected to a number of brief, tantalising but unsuitable glimpses of Watkinson as he moved around the back of the house. He was accustomed to dealing with a shifting target, but the man was proving elusive and with only time for one shot he would have to make it count.

When the cold muzzle of the Walther touched the back of his neck, he froze. A second pair of hands took away the rifle and he was suddenly face down with a knee in the centre of his back. A nylon garden tie secured both wrists and he was frog-marched out of the field and up the back garden.

"Night owl to eagle, over."

"Eagle, go ahead."

"Target acquired. Situation secure. Approaching rear of property, over."

"Roger night owl, come on in. Eagle out."

The man now sitting at the kitchen table before Watkinson was a complete stranger; George would have been amazed at any other alternative. He refused any attempt at conversation and had no means of identification on his person. The equipment he carried, apart from the rifle, could have been purchased at any hardware store and there was no trace of a strange vehicle in the area. They took swabs for DNA comparison and prints from both hands but Watkinson seriously doubted whether he would appear on any database that they could access. The faint smile on the man's face told him that this was just an occupational hazard. He would face a short prison term for possession of a dangerous weapon and then simply disappear. It was the paper that gave him away.

A search of the equipment found beyond the back fence had revealed, in addition to the aforementioned, the information given to the assassin at the commissioning of the job. On first sight it appeared to be no more than clean, standard A4 copy paper but forensic tests revealed a single but very clear fingerprint on the bottom corner. Cross matching against the police database revealed a match to prints taken from man involved in a disturbance outside a Birmingham night club some years before. It was the final break that Watkinson had been hoping for and the chance to finally kill off the organisation.

38

*T*here had been no contact from the contractor since the job had been commissioned, but that in itself was not a cause for worry for Gerald Montgomerey; these things, properly planned could take weeks to set up and carry out. He stared out of the board room window of the engineering company which had been set up by his father Friedrich after the end of the war. Success had been spectacular and fast in the reconstruction years of the fifties, and the personal fortune which the man left had enabled continuance of his vision of the future. The Third Reich had been a wonderful dream for them all, soured by the megalomania into which the inner cabal had descended. As one of the senior army officers after the suicides which took the Nazi leadership away, he escaped to England along the route laid down by Bormann. Bormann had seen the end coming, had fully understood the nature of what was in store for Germany in the aftermath of the holocaust, and had laid down plans to rejuvenate the better parts of the dream in another society.

All that had now been compromised by the fool losing the files in his panic to evade capture. It had taken forty years to get to this point and Mason, another idiot had lost the documents just when it had seemed that the last evidence of the plan could be destroyed. They had been so close and another ten years would have seen a new dawn for Britain and Europe under a strong and vibrant society filled with all that was good.

The country had been dragged kicking and screaming from its status as the sick man of Europe in the late sixties and early seventies, and the communists running the trade union movements had all been consigned to history. Gerald himself had been a staunch supporter of Thatcherism and the country had stood on the brink of something truly great.

He sighed and sat down at the table, picked up his coffee cup and switched on the television. BBC News 24 was running a story which almost made him drop the drink. A stream of police cars was converging on the Birmingham area and reports leaked to the media indicated that a terrorist cell had been located in the Edgbaston area of the city. This had to be George Watkinson, and the full realisation of the failure of the assassination attempt now dawned upon him. He grabbed his car keys and a cloth parcel, and left by the fire exit into the car park. Minutes later he was away and heading north out of the city towards the M1; he would have to ditch the car and took the opportunity to hire a replacement at the first available facility. There was a world of difference between his Daimler and the Mondeo he now drove, but anonymity was the key and the further north he could travel the better would be his chances of escape.

Back at the factory, screeching tyres and burning rubber brought the arrival of the police convoy into the car park, sealing it off completely. A bemused receptionist put through a call to Montgomery's office but received no reply. George Watkinson was up the central staircase with a squad of armed officers and unceremoniously flung open the MD's door. The office was tidy, almost as if no-one had been there all day, but once through the adjoining door into the boardroom he knew that they had been too late. The fire exit was still open and swinging on its hinges; they could have only missed him by minutes, and turning around at the sound of voices he realised why. The television was still on, and an outside broadcast unit had just arrived outside the premises.

"Blast!" he cursed out loud. "Steve! Steve!"

"Sir?"

"Find out who the hell let them know about all this and have that person in my office tomorrow morning. Clear?"

"Yes sir."

Marshall had seen his boss angry before but never quite like this, and made a call to MI5 to set wheels in motion before things got any worse. Watkinson returned to the reception to discover that no-one had seen Montgomery leave but an APB on the registration number of the Daimler quickly revealed a vehicle matching its description speeding away from the city and heading north. Pursuing motorway police had lost the vehicle as it left the M42 and it had not been seen since. By the time a nationwide alert had been issued for him, Gerald had cleared Birmingham and was heading north for Leeds but fate was to conspire against him in the most unfortunate manner. Just north of the Trowell services and approaching junction 26, his right foot suddenly plunged all the way to the floor. Amid a blaring of horns and flashing of lights he lost power and, thinking quickly, ploughed his way across two lanes of traffic and down the slip road towards the A610. Clouds of smoke from under the bonnet told him that something was seriously wrong with the engine and pulling over on to the grass verge he abandoned the now useless vehicle.

Looking around, there was no sign of any police pursuit and he grabbed his coat from the rear seat and made his way down to the main road into Nottingham. With time against him he needed to disappear into the crowd, and flagging down the next available bus took the short trip into the city centre. He was hungry but with no time to spare took the first available taxi to the Midland Station. Having paid the fare he checked his wallet – about four hundred in there and it would have to go a long way if he were to avoid capture. He was not to know it, but Watkinson's men were hard on his heels and had already located the abandoned car. From there it was fairly obvious that he would head for the nearest big city as his best option, and the railway police had already been put on alert.

As the taxi returned to its city centre base, Montgomery strode across the concourse and into the ticket hall. As far as he could ascertain nothing appeared to be out of the ordinary as he bought a ticket north and headed for the platform. The train was not due out for a further twenty minutes and with the barriers still down, he took refuge in the buffet area. He hadn't noticed the gradual clearing of commuters from the immediate area until the figure of an armed and uniformed officer appeared outside. The man was typically kitted out with the equipment of a tactical squad, and Montgomery picked up a discarded newspaper as a means of concealment. It was a case of too little too late, and the movement attracted the attention of the officer.

With only one means of entry and exit he was now trapped unless another way of getting out of there could be found. Looking around he found it. A young woman with an overnight bag was moving past him beckoned by the policeman, but with the gun he had brought from the office in Birmingham now in his hand he grabbed her and held it to her head.

"You!" He yelled at the now stationery officer "Back off! Out! Get out!"

With the platform area now filling up with a mixture of more tactical units and Watkinson's agents. Montgomery's chances of escape were now diminishing by the minute. Still he persisted, and moving slowly forward with the woman clasped tightly before him he made for the door where the assembled police now parted like some human Red Sea. The station buffet was in the left hand corner of the platform area and with no-one to that side, the two of them headed for the train on the end track.

"Get this thing ready to move!" he yelled, and made a show of releasing the safety catch on the pistol. The woman screamed and her knees buckled, dragging them both towards the ground, In the ensuing confusion a loud 'crack' was heard from high up on the other side of the station and Gerald Montgomery slumped to the floor, eyes wide in horror as he clutched his chest.

George Watkinson emerged from a crowd of security staff and ran towards the stricken figure. With blood now pouring from a gaping wound in the middle of his chest, it was clear that Montgomery did not have long to live. Seeing the man responsible for the collapse of the organisation now before him, a smile played its way across the bloodied lips on his face.

"You'll never take me alive, copper" He whispered as a melodramatic cackle escaped from his mouth. Watkinson shook his head in disbelief. With his final breath the man had stolen centre stage not realising that it had been the attack in Surrey which had given him away. Without that last gesture of defiance, MI5 would have had no way of tracing him. His head fell away to one side and he was gone. Steve Marshall took that opportunity to step forward, handing his gun to the nearest officer.

"You'll be needing to get that checked I suppose."

"Not the first time you've come to the rescue, Steve and it probably won't be the last."

Watkinson turned away as the ambulance staff bagged up the body and moved out of the station. Steve Marshall watched his boss return to the squad car outside the station and mused over what he had just done. Montgomery had to be silenced. Taken into custody there was no way of knowing what he would have revealed. His motives were well known to all those within the organisation, but not all shared his altruistic view of a better Britain. It remained to be seen what the remnants of the hierarchy which had escaped the purge would do now that they were relatively safe. The rebuilding could now start in earnest.

39

*I*t was now almost one year to the day when Julie Martin's aunt Molly had died and six months since the death of Gerald Montgomery on Nottingham station. Julie had been reluctant to return to the house in Solihull in the aftermath of Alan Mason's shooting but Doug's persistence had paid off for a while. When the advertisement appeared in a local holiday brochure for the cottage in Tewkesbury however, her eyes brightened with excitement, and three weeks later saw them pulling into the same parking bay which they had used the previous year. Number nine St Mary's Lane was now a holiday let but that made not one scrap of difference to her, it was where she wanted to be. She could almost see Roger Fretwell wiping the perspiration from his forehead as he greeted them on that late spring afternoon and with the property keys clutched firmly in her hand, she led the way up the well-worn pathway to the front door.

Little had changed inside the cottage apart from a modest amount of bringing the property up to modern standards, and the furniture had remained exactly as Roger and Madeline had left it. Clearly the new owner wanted to retain as much of the rural charm as possible. Julie had not realised how big the place actually was until she and Doug carried their bags up the broad staircase. The upper floor comprised a master bedroom and two smaller singles together with a bright and airy bathroom, but their exploring was temporarily interrupted by a knock at the front door. Doug opened it to be greeted by Harry Charlesworth, the owner who had sent them the brochure a few weeks before. They sat down to tea and some cakes which Julie always had ready for occasions such as this, and talked about the property and its history.

Harry and his wife had bought the cottage some six months ago fully intending to retire to the South West, but financial problems had forced them to let it instead, and he freely admitted now that he would not be able to hold on to it much longer. Julie sensed something more, and with a kick to Doug's ankle under the table asked how much they would want for the place if a suitable buyer could be found. Harry Charlesworth was a shrewd man who had been the unfortunate victim of a pension fund collapse, and admitted that it would be difficult for him and his wife to hold out for what they regarded as the true market value when property prices eventually recovered. Doug stepped in with a ridiculously low offer, and over the course of the next half hour they reached an agreement over the price. Julie could hardly contain her excitement after he had gone.

"God, Doug what have we done? What about the house in Solihull? What about the kids?"

"Calm down Jules." He remained, as always, a pragmatic figure. "He might back out when he gets to thinking about it. Don't let's count any chickens."

As if to dispel any uncertainties the phone, a recent addition, rang out an hour later. It was Harry with the news that he and his wife were prepared to accept the Martins' offer if they could complete within a month. Doug agreed without further discussion and a little over three weeks later they were the owners. By the end of the summer the move had been completed and Julie had her dream home in the most beautiful surroundings she could ever have imagined. In one final moment of contentment she sent a photograph to the Fretwells' new home in Cleethorpes with a note telling Madeline that her beloved cottage was in safe hands. Two months later she had more news to tell as a young couple moved into the cottage at the end of the row which had stood empty since the death of old George Murfin. They seemed nice enough but try as she may, Julie could not get them to open up and with a steady flow of friends going in and out of the property neither seemed to have much time for village life.

Correspondence with Madeline and Roger continued for another five years, but a sad note arrived early in February 1998 from their son, Brian. During a spell of particularly unpleasant weather Madeline had caught a chill, and despite staying within the house on the orders of her doctor had deteriorated considerably over the course of a fortnight. She had been in hospital for only a week when she passed away in her sleep. Roger was inconsolable and without Madeline by his side he too slipped away a few weeks afterwards. The letter contained a smaller envelope and Julie recognised it immediately. Tipping the contents out on to the kitchen table she smiled at the yellowing pages of the note written so many years ago; a single tear meandered slowly down the contours of her cheek. Doug picked up a small piece of card from the floor.

"Look at that Julie, he even had it framed."

The train ticket perfectly preserved on a cardboard mount and behind a piece of clear film dropped into her hand.

"Who would have thought that a ticket to Tewkesbury could have been the cause of so much fuss, Doug?"

40

*T*he occupants of number 1, St Mary's Lane had become a fixture in the village, but Julie and Doug had never been able to make any acquaintance with them which extended beyond the nodding of heads in passing. The date is mid 2002, and at a social gathering of a number of friends at the end of the little lane, a stranger who had not been seen there before rolled up in a Bentley. He was tall, fair haired and carried himself with the self-assured manner of someone accustomed to being obeyed without too many questions being asked. He entered the cottage at the end of the row without knocking and Doug frowned from his front garden vantage point at this show of familiarity.

Those inside, however, showed no such concern for the man's manner and all greeted him with the warmth of a long-lost relative. It had been almost ten years since the purging of the organisation from British political circles, and the blows delivered by George Watkinson had been all but fatal to the cause. The intervening time had been that of slow and painstaking progress with meetings held in circumstances of the utmost secrecy, but now there was a hint of light at the end of a very long tunnel.

Steve Marshall, for it was he who had lain the foundations of today's gathering, had kept his role within MI5, managing throughout the years to keep his political activities out of the all-seeing gaze of Watkinson. It had been, at times, an extremely difficult road to travel, but in the years since the general election in 1997 the present government had been coming under increasing pressure in relation to its foreign policy. With an unpopular conflict in the Middle East now looking increasingly likely it would probably be a good time to strike. Those around him were still all fairly young for the onerous mantles which they were about to assume, but he had been in their position himself at one time and was certain that they would cope.

Looking around at their expectant gazes and to paraphrase one particular political cliché, he felt the hand of history resting upon his shoulder as he read from a prepared set of notes. Funds left in a secret bank account by Gerald Montgomery had been more than sufficient to finance the phoenix of a new organisation rising from the ashes of the old, and this time there would be no room for any sentiment. The aims were clear and anyone standing in the way would simply be mown down as the steamroller of progress made its inexorable way forward.

His speech received a rousing reception; outside in the peace of a summer evening, and in his garden, Doug Martin wondered idly at the party atmosphere emanating from the cottage at the end of the row. There had been a series of arrivals from early in the morning, but neither he nor Julie had recognised the occupant of the Bentley. As he passed their garden at the end of the evening, and with the broadest of smiles upon his face, Steve Marshall bade them both 'good night' and drove off into the gathering darkness.